MW00423799

People
of the Horse

A LUKE KASH WESTERN

People
of the Horse

DUKE CHARLES

Copyrighted Material

People of the Horse

Copyright © 2016 by D C Engel. All Rights Reserved.

No part of this publication may be reproduced, stored in a retrieval system
or transmitted, in any form or by any means – electronic, mechanical,
photocopying, recording or otherwise – without prior written
permission from the publisher, except for the inclusion
of brief quotations in a review.

For information about this title or to order other books
and/or electronic media, contact the publisher:

D C Engel

Twin Eagle Promotions

El Paso, TX 79912

www.DukeCharles.com

twineaglepromo@sbcglobal.net

ISBNs

Softcover: 978-0-9969673-0-3

eBook: 978-0-9969673-1-0

Printed in the United States of America

Cover and Interior design: 1106 Design

For my bride and family for always being there.

Foreword

Home, Home on the Range.

Duke Charles truly should have been born about 150 years ago in a home on the range. He is a cowboy to the core—born and bred—spirit to bone. The soul that surrounds him is defined in this story.

His story, *People of the Horse,* will capture you and hold you and will more than likely make you want more Luke Kash—it did me.

This story is an autobiographical dream life of the author. But, the author I know is much older than Luke and surely not so handsome. Duke is a crusty old dreamer. He is a cowboy, a performance artist, a musician, a storyteller. And, he is a wonderful cook—I know first hand.

He was born and raised up near the bottom of California. He spent some time guarding our coast in the U.S. Coast Guard. He spent most of his adult life in El Paso, Texas and claims he is married to the most beautiful woman in the world.

I am honored to have been asked by Duke Charles to introduce his book, *People of the Horse*.

And, if you read this truly good book, I suggest that you will be like me in hoping that we will hear more from Duke Charles and particularly more about the adventures of Luke Kash.

K.B. (Ken) Whitley

Marfa, Texas

Prologue

Bear snarled low.

"I hear him, stay quiet," Luke said softly.

Bear's eyes followed the dark figure as it moved toward the camp. He was in his spot under the seat of the wagon.

"Put yer hands in the air and turn around. And don't try anything or I'll drop ya where ya stand."

Luke turned with his hands up and faced the robber without any fear on his face.

The robber was visibly shaken to see how calm the young man was. He kept his pistol on Luke.

The light coming from the camp fire allowed Luke to see that his shooter was a Colt Peacemaker in need of a good cleaning and some repair.

"What can I do for you?" asked Luke.

"I'll take yer money and yer supplies and be on my way, unless you make me put one of these .45s in yer ass."

"If ya shoot me now all you'll be gitting is about four dollars and a few supplies, and I won't be able to show you where the gold is."

The dark figure's eyes opened wide at the thought of finding gold.

"OK! Where's this gold yer yapping about?" the robber asked.

"Very close, but I'm afraid you'll never see it," Luke said as he moved his right index finger slightly.

The robber looked confused.

Bear leapt from the floorboard of the wagon, and almost two hundred pounds of solid muscle slammed into the man's left side. Bear's rear legs knocked the cocked pistol from his hand, and the big dog's mouth closed around the man's throat. He screamed just before Bear tore the life out of him. By the time he hit the ground, blood was spraying everywhere. His arms and legs flailed uncontrollably in all directions and a noise came from his throat that sounded like a steam engine sucking air, then he suddenly laid still, all signs of life gone forever.

"Bear, back!"

Bear came around behind him and sat at his right heel.

"I guess we'll need to take this one into town in the morning,"

Luke said to Bear, and the large dog made what could only be described as a grunt in agreement.

Luke lay in his bed in the wagon with Star in his arms. He wasn't concerned about security because Bear was by their side.

For a brief moment, Luke thought of the first man he ever killed, then drifted off to sleep.

Chapter 1

Five years earlier . . .

Luke was standing on the front porch of his mom and pa's small ranch house, watching his pa work with a young Appaloosa, the finest horse young Luke had ever seen in his short fifteen years. He was amazed every time he watched his pa work with a new horse, or any animal for that matter; he had a way with all critters. It was like they could read each other's mind.

Jed (Jedediah) Kash was a full-blooded Ute Indian (Ute means "The People of the Horse"). He had moved to a small ranch just west of Taos, New Mexico, when he found that there was a market for good horses. Jed would gentle and train your mount for you or sell you one of his horses. He usually had one or two well-trained horses on the ranch. Jed was a great horseman but he never rode; he preferred to walk everywhere he went.

This particular morning Jed had been working with the Appaloosa that the cattle rancher up the road a couple of miles had brought down. He paid Jed thirty dollars to gentle and train to saddle.

Jed was walking the big horse around the corral to cool it down when he tripped over the extra-long lead rope and fell forward face down just as the big horse's front left hoof came crashing down onto the left side of Jed's head.

The horse knew what had happened and tried to back away, but it was too late.

Luke ran to the corral when he saw his pa go down but he had this terrible sinking feeling in his gut. When he reached the corral, his pa was moaning and trying to speak, but not much sound was coming from his bloody mouth. Luke raised his head and cradled him in his arms.

Jed didn't open his eyes, but Luke heard him say in an almost inaudible voice, "It wasn't his fault, I tripped." Then he passed out. About two hours later Jed died without saying another word or regaining consciousness.

They didn't have many neighbors but a few of the ranchers in the area showed up for the funeral.

The McCrackens up the road who owned the Appaloosa were so sorry. They didn't know what to say, and they didn't have any money to help out Luke or his mother Mary, but they told them to keep the thirty dollars and the big horse.

Two weeks later to the day, around 10:00 P.M., Luke was sleeping on his mat on the floor close to the wall across from the fireplace when he woke to the sounds of his mother sobbing. He saw a man with his back to Luke, his pants down around his ankles, bending his mother backward over their kitchen table.

Luke wasn't sure what was happening. He had seen the livestock act like that, and his pa had tried to explain what was going on, but it didn't make much sense at the time. But now he knew it wasn't good.

He jumped to his feet, grabbed the fireplace poker, and without a thought hit the man in the side of the head just above his right ear. Luke dropped the poker, and the man fell to the wooden floor face down. He stood there staring at the stranger and noticed that the hook on the poker was stuck in the man's head. The man had taken his last breath; a pool of blood started to form under his head.

His mother was crying and having trouble breathing, coughing and spitting up some blood. She told Luke she was fine and not to worry, but Luke knew something was wrong.

Two days later when Luke came in from feeding the stock, the two sheep, two cows, the hog, chickens, and ducks—his afternoon chores—he found his mother sitting in her favorite chair, the rocker, with her Bible in her lap. Luke smiled. He thought she was just praying because she loved her Bible verses and loved to talk with her God. But soon he realized she wasn't breathing; she looked so peaceful and beautiful just sitting there. That's the way Luke would always remember her.

Luke's mother died of internal injuries from the beating she had received from the saddle tramp. She never stopped bleeding inside her belly or her head.

Luke was under the impression that they owned the little ranch, but a few days after his mother's funeral a man showed up saying they were six months behind on the mortgage.

He said he was from the bank and Luke would have to pay up or find another place to live.

Luke had no idea what to do.

By this time Luke had finished gentling and training the big Appaloosa, and they had become fast and inseparable friends. He had named him Storm because when he rode he could feel the fury in his body. Luke had never known an animal with such speed and agility, and he was smarter than most horses.

Unlike his pa, Luke loved to ride. His pa had had him on horseback from the time he was old enough to hold on to a handful of mane, always bareback. But now there was no pa to advise him, no mother to fix his meals or keep his extra set of coveralls and shirt clean; he was on his own.

Chapter 2

The next morning Luke had hitched the ox cart up to Storm and was looking around to see if he had missed anything. He didn't have much: the small table, a couple of chairs, a dresser, a rocking chair his father had made and carved the wildlife and flowers of the valley on—it was a beautiful piece—the six gun, holster, cartridge belt, and Winchester he had kept from the stranger who killed his mother. He had twelve dollars that he took out of the man's pockets, thirty-five dollars he got for selling the stranger's horse and rig, and another five dollars he found in one of the drawers of the dresser as he was loading it on the wagon.

He had picked all the carrots, potatoes, and tomatoes out of his mother's garden, loaded them into toe sacks, and put them in the cart. He had been so busy he almost forgot about the family dog that had been sitting on the porch just watching and waiting for Luke to give him a task.

Skeeter was black and white, about the size of a coyote. He lived to herd, and it didn't matter what: cows, sheep, hogs, ducks or chickens. Luke even saw him bring four frogs right up to the front porch one time and just hold them there till Luke's pa told him what a good dog he was, and then Skeeter let them go on their way.

Luke looked around one more time and couldn't be sure what else belonged to his folks, so he left some things behind: a small bed, some pot and pans, dishes, and some mismatched flatwear.

After a final look around, he decided it was time to go. He opened the gate to the pasture and told Skeeter to fetch 'em up.

It was quite an unusual sight, Luke moving up the trail toward Taos, walking beside this beautiful Appaloosa horse hitched up to an ox cart. Behind them twenty yards or so followed a herd of two cows, two sheep, a hog, eight chickens, and a gaggle of geese all being herded by this black-and-white dog that was in complete control. People passing him by as he got closer to town would just smile and shake their heads.

Luke wasn't sure where he should be going but he knew he couldn't stay at the ranch any longer. It was about a three-hour walk to town. He stopped several times by the stream that wandered along the trail to let Storm and the livestock drink and feed on the lush grass since he wasn't really sure what he might encounter once he made it to town. He didn't want to have to spend his money on feed until he was sure he would have a place to stay.

He came into town from the southwest and took what looked to be an alley on the east side of Taos that ran north to south. They had walked a few blocks when Luke found a real good area just off the path by the same stream they had been following all day. It was a large pasture on the other side of the stream. The pasture was open with no fence; he had Skeeter herd the flock across the stream and hold them there. It was about two in the afternoon when he got all the stock settled. He decided they could spend the night there since Luke had no idea how to go about selling off his herd, and Skeeter had everything under control.

Luke was about half worn-out, not so much from the trail but from the stress of not knowing where he was going or what he might find.

He went down to the stream and waded in, his clothes, boots and all; he liked being clean, something his mother had instilled in him for as long as he could remember. He splashed water on his face and then just sat down in the stream. The water running over his body felt amazing.

He was so caught up in relaxing that he didn't see the middle-aged man and woman standing across the trail watching him intently and smiling to one another.

Luke got out of the stream, pulled off his worn-out old boots, and set them up in the cart. Then he took off his shirt and britches and hung then on one of the side boards to dry. He was just getting ready to crawl under the cart and catch a few winks in the plush grass when he heard a raspy, deep voice from behind him say, "God damn it, boy, what the hell are you doin'?"

He had a strange accent Luke had never heard before. Luke looked up to see this giant of a man in a white apron all stained with blood.

Luke was kinda startled at the harshness of the man's voice. He looked the man in the eye and said, "Sorry, sir, but we been on the trail since about sunup, and I was just takin' a little break. I can move on if there's a problem."

"Where the hell ya comin' from? And where the hell ya headin'?" asked the big man.

"Uh well, I'm comin' from our ranch about six miles from here, and I don't rightly know where I'm headin'," replied Luke.

"How the hell can ya not know where yer headin'?" the giant asked.

"Well, sir, my pa and ma both ended up dead, and a man came by a couple of days ago and told me I'd have to leave. So here I am—uh, I mean, here we are."

"That's quite a god-damn herd ya got there. Can't say I ever seen anything like it before. How the hell do ya keep 'em all rounded up?" the giant of a man asked.

"That's Skeeter's job, and he's pretty good at it, too."

"He sure the hell is, that's fer god damn sure."

About that time the lady came walking over. She was a heavy-set woman who looked to be in her mid-50s with big rosy-red cheeks and a smile that made you want to laugh every time you saw it.

She said, "Joseph, leave that child alone," and she walked up and put her arms around Luke. That made him really uneasy because he was soaking wet and standing there in his long drawers.

"Call me Mama B," she told Luke and he said, "Yes, ma'am."

"Are ya hungry, boy?" she inquired, concerned.

"Well, yeah, I guess I am."

"When was the last time ya ate?" she asked.

Luke thought about it for a second or two and replied, "Had some raw carrots yesterday afternoon."

Mama B took him by the arm and led him straight across the path and into the back door of what turned out to be Johansen's Butcher Shop and Custom Meats.

Mama B sat Luke down at a small table in a room off of the butcher shop and brought him a large plate of the most amazing meats he had ever tasted. He couldn't stop eating long enough to even talk. When he finally cleared his plate, Mama B got up to get him another.

Luke asked, "What did you do to that meat? I've never tasted anything like that in my life."

Mama B smiled that infectious smile and said, "Papa Jo cooks it out back."

About that time, Papa Jo came walking into the room with four big beef ribs on a piece of wood. They smelled wonderful, and the meat was almost ready to fall off the bone.

Papa Jo said, "God damn it, these here are for yer dog, he looks like he can use a good meal."

Luke asked, "Are you sure that's dog scraps? It smells pretty dang good."

Luke heard Skeeter barking, and he got up and rushed outside. He saw a young man on horseback pawing through some of the things in the cart.

Skeeter was growling and barking and getting ready to attack the man, who looked like he was getting ready to pull his pistol.

Luke stepped up to the man just as he started to clear leather, grabbed his right hand, and pulled him from his horse. He landed in the dirt with a thud, and Luke's bare foot on top of his right hand to prevent him from pulling his pistol.

The young man spit and said, "When I get up I'm gonna whup yer ass good!"

Luke asked, "You weren't plannin' on shootin' my dog, were ya?"

The man wasn't as old as Luke had expected, maybe just shy of twenty.

The young man said, "I was thinking hard on it."

"Why would you want to do something like that?" Luke asked. "He was just protecting my stuff."

The young man smiled at Luke as he got up from dirt and brushed the dust from his backside.

"You got some pretty interestin' stuff in there," he said. "You just might have somethin' I can use."

Luke started to get a little perturbed.

"There ain't nothin' in there that's any of yer business."

The young man said, "I usually just take what I want. Ain't no one to stop me around here, so unless yer lookin' for a heap of trouble, more than you can handle, you better just back off."

Luke came up from his side with a slow left hook that he telegraphed on purpose.

The man saw it coming and smiled as he blocked it with his right arm.

He thought to himself, "This kid is a fool." It was the last thing he would think of for a while.

Luke came straight up the middle with a lighting-fast right fist that smashed the man's nose flat against his face. His eyes rolled up under his lids, and he collapsed, hitting the ground once again like a big ol' bag of spuds.

Luke went to the cart and took out a wooden bucket. He walked over to the stream and scooped up a bucket of icy cold water. He stood over the saddle tramp and poured the water over the man's head.

He came up sputterin' and spittin' and cussin', "Ya son of a bitch! Ya broke my nose!"

Luke said, "Nah I didn't. There ain't no bones in yer nose, just cartilage. But I did smash it all over yer face purdy good."

Luke helped him up and onto his horse, then said to him, "You might want to tell me yer name."

The man looked at Luke with confusion on his face. "My name is Danny Collins," he said, as blood ran in a steady stream from his nose down his cheek and on to his shirt. "Why?"

Luke said, "In case I'm ever lookin' for a heap of trouble I'll know who to look up."

Danny Collins spurred his horse and rode off at a slow gallop still cussin', and Luke never saw hide nor hair of him again.

Luke realized that he was still in his long drawers and bare feet, and it made him smile.

Papa Jo walked up and said, "God damn, boy, that was just about the god damnedest thing I ever seen. That was pretty god damn slick."

Luke just smiled and went to get dressed.

As Luke walked toward his cart, Papa Jo said to him, "God damn it, boy, where ya think yer goin?"

Luke just shrugged; he really didn't know. After he got dressed Papa Jo continued, "God damn it, come look at this god-damned shed I got over here. It ain't much but ya could clean it out, and it'll keep ya out of the god-damn weather till ya come up with a plan. And it looks like yer stock will be fine right where they're at."

Luke asked, "Don't I need to get permission for my animals to stay over there?"

Papa Jo said, "Ah hell, don't worry about that."

Luke took the board with the ribs on it out to Skeeter, He snuck a bite on the way and thought, "This sure as heck ain't dog scraps." The dog got a whiff of the meat and could hardly contain himself. Luke sat down in the grass and watched Skeeter devour the meat and clean the bones till they shined in the sun light. And when he was finished, he moved the bones over under a tree and made a pile as if to say, "These are mine and don't even think of comin' for 'em."

Luke turned around to see a friendly looking man in a heavy leather apron with a large wooden box coming his way.

He walked through the stream, set the box down in front of Luke, and stuck out his hand.

"My name in Gunther. I got the livery, blacksmith, and the gun shop next door, and we do some leather work, too. I brung ya some chicken feed and some scraps for yer hog. Looks like yer gonna be spendin' the night."

Luke shook his hand and introduced himself. "They sure have some nice folks around here," Luke thought.

Luke spent the rest of the afternoon cleaning out the shed. It really was a good size room, about ten-by-fourteen feet, and it was the first time in his life that Luke had a space to call his own. He brought in a couple of bales of hay from the barn and then laid a couple old two-by-twelve planks on the hay to make a bed. He hated sleeping on the ground. He put the small chest from the cart in his room. Mama B brought out a stack of sheep skins with the fleece still on to use as a mattress and some clean wool blankets. The stress started to ease, and Luke could feel the knots in his body start to release.

That evening at dinner Mama B served more incredible tasting meat, something she called sausages. Luke found them so good he couldn't explain the sensation in his mouth.

She had potatoes fried in a big cast iron skillet with onions and some spices that Luke had never heard of or tasted. He asked about every one of them, and he was eager to learn about all the new things that were coming his way. Mama B was happy to explain.

She had fried squaw bread, too, Luke's favorite thing in the world. His mother made the best, he thought, but this was even better. How was that possible? She set a bowl of fresh butter on the table. Luke had never had a meal like this, and things just kept getting better and better for him.

They talked for several hours after dinner, and Luke explained about the death of his pa and mother, his pa's people to the north, and about his mother, who was a school teacher from Philadelphia who had come out West for a change of scenery after her husband had been killed in a logging accident. The stagecoach she was traveling in was robbed, leaving her with just the clothes on her back.

The closest town was Taos, New Mexico. She got a job at the general store for two meals a day and a place to sleep on the floor at the back by the store room. And that's where she met Jed Kash. He studied her for some time and decided to let her stay at the ranch until she could get on her feet.

She just kinda stayed on; it seemed natural. He told the couple about his mother spending hours every evening by a coal oil lamp teaching him his numbers and to read and write.

Luke looked forward to the evenings with his mother, and he was a very quick study with a hunger for knowledge. He told them about his father and what a gentle man he was, never raising his voice or using a cuss word. Luke told them of how his father had taught him about the Indian ways, how to use a bow and a tomahawk, how to hunt, and how to shoot a rifle and pistol.

Luke didn't realize it, but he had been talking for the best part of four hours. It was close to ten thirty, way past workin' folks' bed time. He really liked these people. Neither he nor the old couple were used to being up this time of night.

As he got up to go to bed, Mama B handed Luke a fresh bun. He was sitting on his bed roll when he took a bite. His eyes shot wide open with surprise as he got the taste of wild berries in his mouth. It was wonderful and things just kept getting better and better, at least for now.

Chapter 3

Luke slept a hard and restful sleep; he had never had a bed that was this soft and comfortable. Awakening just at sunrise completely rested, he dressed quickly and walked out to the meadow. He saw Skeeter lying by his pile of bones and keeping watch over his flock. His tail began to wag as Luke approached.

Luke walked through the stream and up to Storm. The big horse snickered and rubbed his muzzle against Luke's chest, and Luke scratched his neck and jaw.

Luke was only fifteen but he stood almost six feet in his stockings, and he still had some growing to do. But the fact was he didn't own a pair of stockings.

Storm was an extremely large horse and Luke usually stood on a stump or large rock to climb aboard. But he couldn't see anything he could use close by, so he jumped as hard as he could and landed on his stomach on the back of the big horse. Storm stayed perfectly still while Luke settled himself.

He just touched Storm's flanks with the heels of his boots, and the big horse responded by going into a slow gallop. Luke touched him again and Storm started to run full out. The boy sat his back like he was glued to it, horse and rider in complete and perfect unison.

Papa Jo was standing at the back door. He called to his wife, "Hey, mama! God damn it, come look at this. You ain't gonna believe what the hell ya see."

She came to the door, and they stepped outside.

"Look at that god damned boy settin' that big horse just like a God damn Injun. Just like he was born there. He don't have a damn saddle or bridle or a damn thing, they just seem to know what the other one wants to do. God damndest thing I ever seen."

Luke rode for about thirty minutes, and Storm didn't even break a sweat. He walked him down and stopped him in the stream to let him drink. Then he walked him out of the stream, dropped the reins of the soft rope hackamore on the ground, and walked back to join Mama B and Papa Jo for breakfast.

Mama had more of the warm buns with berries inside along with butter, scrambled eggs, and smoked ham.

Luke just shook his head in amazement. "What food!" he thought to himself. While they were eating, Mama B poured them hot coffee unlike the mud he was used to, and Papa Jo said, "God damn it, Luke. Me and ma been talkin' and, well, we want you to think about somethin'."

Luke listened, not knowing what to expect.

Papa Jo started, "We want ya to stay with us, and I'm willin' to butcher your stock and split the profit with ya when we sell the meat. Oh yeah, and you can keep the god damn skins to sell or whatever you want to do with 'em, and we'll give ya some chores to do around here and pay ya a dollar a week. Whatdaya think?"

Luke wasn't sure he heard him correctly. He muttered, "Uhhh, yer gonna give me a place to sleep, my meals, and pay me a dollar just to help around here—is that right?"

Papa Jo smiled and said, "Hell yes, by golly that's right."

Luke was so excited he blurted out, "WHY HELL YES!" When he realized what he said, he turned bright red. He had never used a swear word of any kind in his entire life. He apologized to Mama B.

She just smiled and said, "Ah, don't worry, that old man's bad habits will just wear on ya."

Papa Jo got up and went to start his day now that he had some meat to butcher and sell. As Luke helped Mama B clear the dishes, she just smiled; she knew they had made the right decision.

"Can I ask you a question?" Luke asked.

She gave Luke a confused look.

"Why, of course, boy, what is it?"

Luke wasn't sure how to approach the subject so he just jumped right in.

"How come it is that Papa Jo cusses so much?"

She smiled and answered, "When papa first came to the new country he took a job as a cook for a large cattle ranch up north around Denver. They had lots of cowboys, and they all cussed a blue streak. That's where papa learned to speak English. He don't mean nothing by it. In fact, he don't even know he does it most of the time."

Luke said, "The only time I ever heard any talk like that was once in a blue moon when my mother got really upset, once or twice a year, and then she always said she was sorry."

After helping Mama B clean the dishes, Luke went out to his cart and started hauling the sacks of vegetables out of his mother's garden so the Johansens could sell them in the butcher shop. Mama B just smiled; she did that a lot.

Chapter 4

Over the next few weeks Luke worked in the butcher shop and the customers loved him. He almost always got a tip because he would carry out their packages of meat and put them in their wagons. They weren't used to that kind of service. And he didn't cuss. Word was spreading about the new kid in town.

Not too long after that, Luke came up with the idea of putting a chalk board out front so the customers would know what kind of meat would be available the next day. That way, they could order what they wanted and pay in advance. Papa Jo loved that idea.

Luke would hook up the ox cart to Storm and deliver the orders every afternoon. He always had about ten deliveries and got a tip at each farm, ranch, or small home in town, a dime, quarter, or sometimes a bag of eggs or vegetables or even fruit.

He would bring everything back and give it to Mama B. It never entered his mind that he could keep the money he got as tips.

Mama B would sell the fruit and vegetables to the town folk and business was booming.

Luke learned about smoking meat in the small metal oven out back. He noticed some of the meat would burn or get dried out because they weren't able to control the heat, and that gave him an idea: move the oven over and use it for a fire pit. Build a much bigger oven, about six feet high, four feet wide, and four feet deep, with shelves on the inside and a door on the front with a latch. Then run a pipe from the fire pit to the new smoker oven. That way, they could keep the direct heat away from the meat.

Papa Jo listened to his idea with amazement; he knew it would work. He called Gunther from the blacksmith shop over to hear Luke's idea. Gunther said it could be done and that he'd get to work on it at once.

Three days later, in the morning while Luke and the Johansen's were having breakfast, they heard a racket coming from out back.

Gunther and his son Hans were moving the new smoker oven into place. He had made the pipe to run from the old oven that was now used just for fire to the new oven so only the controlled heat and smoke could come through. Gunther was leveling the new oven and making it solid in place. Luke was looking it over when he realized that there needed to be a way to control the heat in the main oven.

He mentioned this to Gunther, who took his hat off and scratched his head. Then he smiled and said, "I got it, a chimney with an adjustable flue."

Four hours later they had the new smoker fired up and running. Right away Papa Jo realized there would be no more waste: the meat that didn't sell in the butcher shop during the day would go straight to the smoker, and it would be preserved to be sold in the next few days. A week or so after that Luke was watching the smoke come out of the chimney at the back of the new smoker oven, and it seemed to him that the smoke should be used for something.

He called Papa Jo out and told him his new idea. Three days later the carpenters were putting the finishing touches on a walk-in log smoke house. They were putting meat hooks into two walls, shelves along the other two walls, and stands in the middle of the room. Every inch of space was used. Gunther was extending the chimney from the smoker to the new smoke house. Papa Jo realized he could now have the hunters, ranchers, and farmers bring their livestock and game in for butchering and offer to smoke part or all of their orders.

One day Papa Jo came to Luke and said, "By golly God damn it, boy, you been here awhile and you ain't asked fer no damn money. What the hell is wrong with yer ass?"

Luke just smiled and said, "I don't have a need for any money, I got everything I need."

"You remember we agreed you were gonna get a damn dollar a week?"

"Yeah."

"Well, I changed my mind."

"Did I do something wrong?" Luke asked with great trepidation.

Papa Jo handed him a deerskin pouch, and it was very heavy.

Luke wasn't sure what to think.

Papa Jo said, "Well, god damn it, by golly! Open it!"

Luke pulled the rawhide ties and looked into the pouch. He couldn't believe his eyes. There were all denominations of gold coins, three-dollar, five-dollar, twenty-dollar double eagles. He even saw a fifty dollar liberty piece. Luke had no idea what to say; he had never seen that much money in his life.

He said to Papa Jo, "This can't be right!"

"Oh it's right, by golly," Papa Jo assured him. "You earned every damn bit of it. You have turned our business into a very profitable operation, and this is yours."

Luke took a couple of twenty-dollar double Eagles and a couple of five-dollar gold pieces out of the pouch and asked Papa Jo, "Would you go to the bank with me and help me open an account?"

Papa Jo just smiled. That afternoon Luke met Mr. Weathers the bank manager.

Chapter 5

The next day after Luke had finished his chores he made a beeline for the general store, two shops down. He bought two pair of socks, a new pair of brown denim pants, two new shirts, and a pair of boots made of the softest leather he had ever seen. He thought of buying a belt but didn't want to spend the money. He didn't wear any of his new things; he took them to his room and packed them away in the small dresser.

That afternoon when he had finished his chores he walked over to the livery and blacksmith shop, grabbed a broom, and started cleaning. Gunther didn't say a word, he just smiled to himself and thought, "What a boy."

When Luke had the area sparkling clean and the stalls mucked out, Gunther asked Luke to follow him.

He led Luke through a large door on the other side of the blacksmith shop to a room that Luke had no idea was even there. They walked in and Luke looked around in amazement. He saw guns everywhere: shotguns, rifles, and pistols in holsters all hanging on hooks on the wall. Luke was so stunned by the sight he didn't notice the old man sitting at the large table working on a holster and cartridge belt. There was another table with a saddle and all kind of skins piled on it. They looked like they had been tanned and appeared really soft. Luke walked over and touched one of the hides—even the skins his pa had tanned were nowhere near this soft. "Amazing," he thought.

Gunther got Luke's attention and said, "Luke, this is Miguel Soto. He is a gunsmith and the leather man. He's an artist with anything made out of leather, and he can build a gun out of a rock if you give him a day or two."

Luke shook Miguel's hand, and Miguel's face lit up.

"I have heard much about you Señor Luke, it is my honor for to know you."

Luke smiled back at the man and said, "Thank you, I'm very glad to meet you, too, Mr. Soto."

Miguel said, "No! Please, call me Miguel."

Luke knew they would grow to be very good friends.

Miguel's shop was squeaky clean, his clothes were spotless, and his fingernails were clean and trimmed. Luke had never seen a man so clean and he liked it. He thought of his mother and the way she always kept things extra clean, and he smiled.

The next afternoon after Luke finished his chores, he headed up the trail to an old wagon that had been deserted not far from the butcher shop.

He began to disassemble it, taking the best of the planks and making a bridge across the stream out back so Mama B could walk to the pasture without getting her feet wet.

As it turned out Papa Jo and Mama B owned all the land from the path all the way up the hill and into the forest, and about a half-a-mile in both directions—several thousand acres—in addition to the property on which stood both Gunther's livery and smithy shop and the gun and leather shop, in addition to the buildings on the other side of the butcher shop. It turned out that Papa Jo was quite the businessman. He could see that Luke also had a very good head for business and paid attention to what Luke had to say.

Luke planted a garden with seeds he found at the general store since land was no longer an issue. He planted tomatoes, carrots, potatoes, cabbage, and some things he had never heard of: cucumbers, green beans, and peas. He loved the way Mama B prepared foods. She canned tomatoes and dried carrots, potatoes, and onions. When she put them in water they came back to life and tasted almost fresh. He couldn't wait for the garden to come in to see what the new vegetables would taste like. Every day he checked the garden to see the progress.

Chapter 6

Luke had turned sixteen and had been with Papa Jo and Mama B almost a year, and he truly loved his life. But something bothered him, and he had a feeling he needed to go and see his pa's people. He wasn't sure how the Johansens would take the news so he just jumped right in, as had come to be his style. Mama B looked surprised, but Papa Jo said he had been expecting it and he understood.

Two days later, just after daybreak, Luke was checking his gear. He didn't have much, and he was traveling light. The trip to his pa's people always took his pa and him about three-and-a-half days of hard walking from sunup till sundown. But with Storm he figured about a day, maybe another half day at most. He had his new brown denim britches, a new shirt, new socks, and his new boots on, and he was eager to get on the trail. He had his Winchester rifle, and Miguel had helped him make a leather strap that Miguel stamped with all kinds of animals. Luke thought it was a work of art. Plus, now he could sling it over his head and right shoulder. Miguel had also made him a large leather pouch that was about eighteen inches square and about six inches wide with a large flap that came from the top all the way down to the bottom in front so none of his belongings would spill out. He hung it over his right shoulder, and it rode on the inside of his left hip.

Mama B had packed his favorite foods, six buns with fresh berries baked inside, five large pieces of fried squaw bread each of which Mama B had split open and filled with a different kind of smoked meat and wrapped individually in butcher paper. He absolutely loved what she did with food. The pouch had two compartments, the food was in one and the second held two dozen cartridges for his Winchester. From his bed he had taken a very large wool blanket that was rolled up and tied with rawhide straps. It lay across Storm's withers.

He had kissed Mama B on her bright red cheeks and shaken hands with Papa Jo, who had pulled him close and given him a big hug that caught Luke off guard. Luke was just getting ready to climb aboard Storm when Gunther and Miguel came striding up.

They both had big grins on their faces. Gunther spoke first.

"Luke! We wanted to say goodbye and travel safe, and Miguel has a little something fer ya."

Miguel brought his hands out from behind his back to reveal a custom-made cartridge belt with a large and beautiful tooled sheath built into it. The cartridge spaces were filled with bullets for his Winchester. It was amazing. Luke had never seen any leather work that compared to it. He shook Miguel's hand and said, "Thank you, my friend," and Miguel beamed with pride.

When Luke went to shake Gunther's hand, he brought out his right hand from behind his back and laid the most beautiful-looking knife in Luke's hand, grip first.

Gunther said, "That sheath ain't much good if'n ya ain't got nothin' to fill it up."

Luke looked at the knife; it was polished to perfection, sharp as a razor, and he could see his reflection in the fourteen-inch blade. That's when he noticed the engraving in some kind of beautiful lettering he'd never seen before along the top of the blade. Luke read, "Property of Luke Kash." Luke also noticed that the top edge of the blade from about the middle all the way back to the grip was jagged, and he asked Gunther about its purpose. Luke thought he knew, but he had never seen anything like it on a knife.

Gunter said it was a saw, which made perfect sense.

It was better than any Christmas Luke ever had, and he knew he had everything he needed to survive this trip. He had never had friends like this; the thought of them warmed him inside.

He put his new knife in his sheath and buckled the cartridge belt on. It fit like a glove. He finished sayin' his goodbyes, kissed Mama B, jumped up on Storm, and headed north up the path behind the butcher shop toward the main trail and on to a new adventure.

Chapter 7

Luke had been on the trail about three hours traveling steady but not as fast as he expected to. There was just too much to take in, and he didn't want to miss a thing. He headed Storm over to the stream that ran along the trail, jumped down, and sat in the grass while the big horse drank.

He wished Skeeter had been able to come along. He would have enjoyed the company, but the dog was over twelve years old and really starting to show his age in the last few months. Besides, Mama B had really taken a liking to the old dog, and vice versa.

Skeeter just wanted to stay beside the rocking chair Luke had given her and which she fell in love with. Skeeter knew there was always plenty of good food if he stayed close.

When Luke saw that Storm was finished drinking, he let him eat some of the sweet grass that grew by the stream. Luke looked at the big horse and thought how lucky he was to own an animal like this. Most men would go through their entire life and not have a horse like Storm. Storm was marked like no horse Luke had ever seen; from his head down his neck, across his chest, and all down his body he was so black he almost looked blue. His long and flowing main was white as snow, while just ahead of his rump he turned white with black spots about the size of a man's fist all over his hind quarter. His back legs from the hock down to the hooves were black-like high stockings, and his tail was long and black and almost dragged the ground.

Storm was through eating. He looked at Luke and snickered, indicating he was ready to go. Luke jumped up on his back and touched him gently in the flanks. Storm shook his head in approval, and they were off, continuing north. They crossed the Rio Grande River at a shallow area that looked like animals and wagons had crossed in the past but not recently.

He rode close to a small town called Tres Piederas. Luke could see some of the buildings a mile or so in the distance, but he decided to keep on going because he really wanted to get back to the wilderness where he felt the most at home.

Every year when Luke and his father went back to his father's people, The People of the Horse, they would spend most of their time in the forest just a couple of hundred yards from the village. Jed preferred camping in the woods by the stream instead of sleeping in the lodges in the village. Luke just felt more at home in the woods except for the part where he had to sleep on the ground. Someday when he was grown he would find a way to never sleep on the ground again.

The trail was plainly marked, and Luke noticed landmarks that he had seen many times with his pa, so he knew he was heading in the right direction. Luke touched Storm again with the heels of his boots, the horse changed his gait to a fast gallop, and the miles began to fly by. They stayed on the trail with the forest several hundred yards to their left. Storm could keep this pace up indefinitely.

Luke had never seen him tire. A few hours later near sundown, Luke reined Storm in to an area where he and his pa had camped many times. It was about six hours hard walking from the home-lands of the Ute nation and Luke's grandparents, and he figured he could make it in about two hours on horseback the next day.

He moved Storm down to the stream and let him drink his fill then brought him up by a tree that was about fifteen feet from where Luke would make his fire. There were still stones laid down for the fire pit from the last time someone had camped here. He dropped the soft rope reins of the hackamore on the ground and let Storm free graze. He knew he wouldn't wander off.

Luke sat by the fire with his back up against a large log, his heavy wool blanket around his shoulders. He was enjoying one of Mama B's stuffed squaw breads. It was filled with smoked chicken and was amazing. He enjoyed another bun with berries then walked down to the stream and washed his face and drank. He relieved himself on a flat rock, giggling when the moisture sprayed in all directions. Then he walked back, sat down against the log near the fire, set his rifle at his side, and quickly fell off to sleep.

When Luke awoke, he wasn't sure how long he had been asleep, but he heard Storm stomping one of his front feet and snickering, so he knew there was a problem.

Just as Luke stood, he saw the large gray wolf jump and fly through the air at Storm's hind quarters. The wolf had no idea what he was in for.

Storm was up on his front feet and met the charge with his rear legs. The large animal had bright shiny teeth, yellow saliva and foam dripping from his mouth, and eyes that looked like they were on fire. He was about two feet from landing on Storm's back when the big horse let his rear feet fly so fast that Luke wasn't sure he saw it. The big horse hit the wolf in the chest with one hoof and in the snout with the other. Luke heard the wolf cry out as he flew through the air back from whence he had come. He hit the ground like an animal that had been shot at close range with a big bore gun, dead in a pile.

Luke knew there were more than just one since they never hunted alone. He started to move back toward the log for his rifle, but before he could reach it another wolf came at him from his right. Luke pulled his knife, and the wolf stopped in front of Luke for just a split-second, then jumped. Luke saw the opening, and with a backhand motion severed the wolf's throat. The knife went through the wolf's skin, muscle, cartilage, and neck bone with absolutely no resistance. Luke had just enough time to raise his left arm as another wolf on his right leapt and grabbed his left shirt sleeve, just nicking the skin with his teeth. The wolf hung in midair with his neck exposed just long enough for Luke to slash from his right side and the big beautiful knife did its job once more.

Luke looked in both directions and grabbed his Winchester. Then he dropped his knife to the ground and chambered a cartridge into the breech of his rifle just as a large black male wolf came charging from the darkness to his left. Luke swung to his left and didn't even aim as he fired from his hip. He hit the big black animal dead in the middle of his chest. Luke cocked, chambered, and fired another round into the wolf's heart before he hit the ground, dead as a doornail.

Luke quickly looked around and then looked at Storm, who was standing patiently waiting for Luke to tell him what to do next. There isn't one horse in ten thousand that would stand there without any fear when there were wolves in the area. Horses are deathly afraid of them. Not so with Storm. He walked over to the wolf he had kicked, smelled it a couple of times, and then did something Luke never would have believed if he hadn't see it with his own eyes. Storm raised his right foot, stomped the wolf's head one time, and casually walked away. He looked at Luke and snickered.

Just about that time Luke heard a growl from the darkness off to his left, about fifteen feet behind the log that Luke had been resting against. He saw two eyes shining through the darkness and reflected by the campfire.

Luke had already chambered another shell into his rifle, and he started walking straight toward the yellow eyes. The wolf stood its ground and then thought better of it and moved off to Luke's left. This had to be the leader of the pack, Luke thought. The one he had shot was large, but this one was half again the size of the other wolf. Luke aimed, squeezed the trigger, and the gun bucked a little as the bullet flew from the barrel, hitting the wolf right behind his left shoulder and tearing out his heart. The big animal dropped straight to the ground without a sound. Luke knew that the Utes hunted wolves to trade with the white men at the fort but had no idea what value they had.

"I have no way to carry them so I guess we won't find out this time," he said to Storm, and the big horse snickered.

It took about two hours before Luke was sure there was nothing more to worry about; he leaned against the log and drifted off to sleep.

Chapter 8

Luke woke at daylight to the sound of Storm snickering, not a sound of distress but almost like he was happy and wanted to play. Luke focused his eyes. Storm had moved closer to the stream, and Luke was amazed to see what looked to be a young bear cub sitting on its haunches right under Storm's muzzle.

Storm's nose was down and the cub's head was held up high; they were licking each other's faces.

Luke just watched for a couple of minutes as they kissed. Storm would move to the left, almost prancing on his front legs, and then to the right, finally coming to settle right over the cub. They would start licking each other's faces once more.

Luke's curiosity finally got the best of him, and he slowly moved toward the pair. He got to within ten feet of them, sat down in the grass, and just watched.

That's when he realized it wasn't a bear cub: it moved too quickly. It was a dog, a pup, and seemed to be about four or five months old, but it was huge. Its paws were already the size of Luke's fists. He sat and watched for another thirty seconds, then the very large pup noticed him and sprung without warning, hitting Luke in the chest with both of his large front feet. The air from Luke's lungs rushed out of his mouth, and he fell backward onto the ground, his eyes closing momentarily. When he opened them he was staring into the face of a giant puppy. His tongue hung out and saliva dripped all over Luke's face. Then the great beast began to lick and lick till Luke felt like the skin on his face may just come off.

It was all Luke could do to push the monster off him. He playfully romped, the way puppies do, almost out of control with his big feet flying in all directions. Then he ran back over to Storm, and they started licking each other once more.

Luke hadn't noticed but about 150 yards away just across the trail, three Indians sat cross-legged with their rifles on their laps and their horses standing behind them with their reins on the ground. Luke finally saw the three men, and he had to look twice to be sure. It was his uncle, Wild Rider, and his two cousins Grey Wolf and White Horse. Luke waved for them to come into the camp, and they started walking forward with big grins on their faces.

Luke's uncle Wild Rider spoke first.

"Well, Walks with Bears, looks like you have yerself a new dog!" he said, and the three Indians chuckled.

"What the hell are you three doing here, and how long have you been setting over there?"

"We got here about two hours before daylight."

"But how did you know I was coming?" asked Luke, confused.

"The old lady, your grandmother, told us last night. She said the spirits told her and we should come and bring you home, so . . . here we are."

Luke greeted his two cousins with a traditional Indian hug. One of them said, "Looks like you made yerself a pot full of money last night."

Luke wasn't sure what he meant.

The young Indian said the gray wolves are worth fifteen dollars each, but the big blacks are worth a hundred dollars apiece, maybe more.

Luke replied, "I don't have any way to get them back to the village."

Wild Rider said not to worry, his sons would skin them and bring them in.

Wild Rider said "We need to ride. Your grandparents are anxious to see you; it has been almost two years. And I see you don't walk anymore. That is a very special long horse you have there. How long can he run?"

Luke replied, "I'm not sure. I always give out before he does."

Wild Rider was impressed. They mounted up and rode to the north, keeping the forest to their left for about three hours. Luke kept an eye on the pup, which hadn't moved from Storm's side since they left camp.

Wild Rider said, "What happened to Skeeter?"

Luke explained that he was getting old and that he had a good home with the Johansens in Taos.

Wild Rider said, "This one is very special. I have never seen a pup this size. What are you going to name him?" and Luke just smiled and said, "Bear . . . . What else?"

They were about a mile from the village when Luke's uncle said, "Let's see if that bag of bones of yours can run." He kicked his paint horse in the flanks and took off at a dead run.

Luke could feel Storm wanting to follow, but Luke gently held him back and talked to him, saying, "Easy boy, you'll get your chance." Wild Rider was almost out of site when Luke said, "OK, big guy, it's your turn."

Storm snickered and tossed his head in the affirmative. Luke touched his flanks gently with his heels and loosened the rope reins to give Storm his head.

"Well alright, let's go get 'em!" Luke encouraged, and Storm jumped forward, almost losing Luke off his back even though he was prepared.

Luke had never felt that kind of power in his life. In three strides Storm had reached full speed, and Luke could not believe how fast the big horse could run. It had only been a matter of seconds before Luke could already tell they were gaining on Wild Rider. Luke looked down and to his right and saw Bear running stride for stride with Storm. Luke could swear he looked like he was smiling.

Luke decided there was nothing to do except to bend over, put his head down low on Storm's neck, and hold on. Storm ran like the wind, never missing a step, and his gait was so smooth that Luke felt like he was floating on air. They had only been running four or five minutes, and Storm was closing the gap between the two horses. The village was still a good three-quarters-of-a-mile away. Luke knew his horse was fast but this was a special kind of fast, and his mind was filled with all the possibilities that came with owning an animal with this kind of ability.

Luke looked up. They were gaining on Wild Rider and closing the gap with every stride the great horse made. By the time they were about a quarter mile from the village, Storm and Luke pulled up even with Wild Rider and his paint pony, who was foaming at the mouth and breathing heavily.

Luke said, "Thanks for waitin' for me," and laughed. Wild Rider looked over at Luke and laid his crop to his horse's rump, but the horse was already giving 100 percent and had nothing left. Luke smiled at Wild Rider and said to Storm, "All right my brother, let's take it home." Storm changed to an even faster gait, and they flew on by the other horse and rider.

Luke looked down with amazement to see Bear still right beside Storm's front feet and having the time of his life. He thought this was the best game ever.

They rode into camp a full two minutes before his uncle Wild Rider and Storm slid to a stop and stood there like he had just finished a leisurely walk around the village; there were no visible signs of sweat on him anywhere.

A young boy came up with amazement on his face. "You just beat the fastest horse in our village," he said. He took Storm's reins and Luke said, "Give him water and the best grain you have and wipe him down. Treat him like the very special horse that he is."

Bear walked off right beside his new companion.

Wild Rider rode up and jumped down from his mount.

"That is one amazing horse you have there, my nephew, and that pup is just as fast."

Luke smiled and said, "Yeah, I guess they do make a pretty good pair."

Chapter 9

uke walked up to his grandparents' lodge and went in. It was larger than most because his grandmother was the shaman and had status among the tribe.

Dark Moon was beaming with joy. She hugged him and kissed his face, and tears came to her eyes.

"We have missed you, my son. I watched you ride like the north wind. It was a great sight. If only your father was alive to see you grow into a great warrior and horseman, he would be so proud."

"How did you know my pa had died?"

She replied, "I knew the minute it happened."

Luke's grandmother handed him a bundle wrapped in a soft deer skin. He was sure he knew what it was. Every year when he and his pa would visit the village, she would have a new set of buckskins and moccasins. And about six or eight months later he would grow out of them. This set was beautiful, with fringe and beads, and they were cut a little larger so as Luke finished growing they should still fit.

"Thank you, grandmother," he said as he admired the gifts.

"Change your clothes and get ready for the celebration," she said.

"What celebration?" asked Luke.

"The return of Walks with Bears. Your grandfather Charging Buffalo will be back from hunting soon, and he will want to see you."

Luke walked down by the lake where Storm and Bear stood in the grass. Storm shook his head and snickered when he saw Luke, and Bear came bounding over.

Luke moved just in time to avoid being knocked off his feet. "Bear! Sit!" he ordered, and low and behold the large pup came up to Luke, dropped down on his haunches, and looked up at Luke with his big tongue out and his tail wagging.

Luke said, "You are a smart one, aren't ya?"

Bear and Storm ran and played as Luke bathed in the icy waters of the crystal clear lake.

Luke's grandfather and the rest of the hunting party returned with their game. They handed the venison, elk, rabbits, and two antelope over to the women at the cook fires. Luke's grandfather

Charging Buffalo spotted him as he was walking back from the lake with Storm and Bear walking close behind. The old man headed down the hill to meet Walks with Bears. They met halfway and hugged.

Luke's grandfather beamed as he gazed at Luke and said, "Look at you. You are a man, my son, and your animals, they are devoted to you. You are a lucky man. Most men live their whole lives and never have animals this fine."

They walked and talked as they moved toward the lodge. Luke felt like a new man in his buckskins and moccasins.

Luke's cousins rode in to the village about thirty minutes before sundown. They greeted Luke and handed him a pouch with six fifty-dollar gold coins. Luke was shocked.

"What is this for?" he asked.

White Horse replied, "The grays were worth twenty dollars each, and the blacks were worth one hundred and twenty each."

Luke looked amazed and tried to split the money three ways among his cousins and himself, but they refused saying they had no use for the white man's coins.

But Grey Wolf said that he would be glad to take that big horse off his hands, and White Horse said he would gladly take the young dog.

Luke smiled and said they better take the money because there was no chance of them getting his animals.

Luke put his arms around both their shoulders, and they laughed and walked together to the feast.

There were a hundred or more tribe's people at the celebration. Luke remembered most of them from two years earlier when he and his pa were last there, but there were a half dozen young girls he did not recognize. They had obviously turned into very pretty young women since the last time he had been in the village, and Luke was aware that they were paying close attention to him and giggling among themselves.

They would turn away when they thought he was looking their way. But there was one young woman Luke could not seem to keep his eyes off of, and she seemed to be looking at him and smiling. She was beautiful, and Luke was in love, he thought.

Luke filled his wooden bowl with an assortment of the different meats and a large piece of fried squaw bread and joined his grandparents, his uncle and his wife, and their two sons. They ate and visited and enjoyed each other's company, but Luke couldn't keep from looking at the maiden. After every one had retired for the night, Luke refilled his bowl with a large amount of venison and some bones that were lying by the cook fire and headed back to the side of his grandparents' teepee where Storm was ground reined. Bear was not far away, either. Luke sat on the ground and said softly, "Bear," and he immediately came to sit at Luke's side. Luke fed him copious amounts of meat and then handed him the large leg bones. Bear moaned and rolled on his back with the large bone in his huge mouth, and he was in ecstasy.

Later that evening as Luke was returning to his grandparents' lodge, he picked up several pieces of charcoal from around the nearest cook fire as he headed off to bed. He lay on the buffalo robe that covered his sleeping area. Picking up a small rabbit skin that had been tanned, he began to sketch with the charcoal. He finally drifted off to sleep and dreamed of a beautiful Indian maiden.

Chapter 10

The next morning Luke woke at sunrise. He dressed, walked out, and stood beside Storm. The big horse put his muzzle against Luke's chest as he stroked his neck and face, and Bear came up to Luke's side for some affection as well. Luke obliged.

Luke jumped up on Storm, and the three of them rode off at a fast gallop to no place in particular. They rode for several hours, enjoying the forest and the fresh air and the abundance of animals that Bear found irresistible. Each time he saw any movement he would jump in that direction, run for ten or twelve feet, and then turn and head straight back to Storm's side. They returned to the village and there was lots of activity.

Luke's grandmother Dark Moon was waiting for him when he arrived back in camp; she had a rabbit skin in her hand.

"Did you do this?" she asked.

Luke said yes, and his grandmother continued, "That's an amazing likeness of Morning Star."

Luke told her that he had been thinking of her since last night at the feast and couldn't get her out of his head.

"Please don't tell her," he pleaded

The old lady smiled and said it may be a little late: everyone in the village had seen it by an hour after sunup. Luke blushed and said, "I guess I should go and face the crowd."

Dark Moon said, "They want you to draw pictures of their children."

Luke saw Morning Star waiting as he walked from the teepee. He said to himself, "Well, I guess I'm in trouble. Or maybe she really wants to talk to me." He walked up and said, "Hey!"

And she said, "So you're more than just a great horseman?"

"Well, I'm tryin', but I'm not exactly sure what I am yet."

They made small talk for a few minutes, and then Luke asked, "Do you ride?" And he immediately thought "DAMNED! That was stupid!"

She said, "Uh, People of the Horse, remember?"

He said "Yeah" and started to blush. "What I meant was, would you like to go for a ride with me?"

"Yes, I would."

Luke said, "Get your horse and let's go."

"I want to ride on that amazing horse of yours. I'll get some food and meet you back here in a few minutes."

He reached down, grabbed her left wrist, and she grabbed his. He swung her up behind him on Storm, and they moved off at a slow gallop with Bear following a step or two behind. They rode for a few miles and found a beautiful spot by a stream that ran down from the mountain. The water was clear and ice cold, coming from the melting snow just six or seven hundred yards up the mountain. Storm and Bear drank and the big horse grazed in the sweet grass by the water.

Luke and Morning Star talked and ate squaw bread and meat from last night's celebration. They laughed and lost track of time. Luke didn't know how long they had been sitting there when he heard Storm snicker and paw the dirt; he did not sound happy. Bear began to growl and then barked several times. Luke jumped to his feet, grabbed his Winchester, and told Morning Star to stay back as he ran to be with his animals. Along the way he cocked and chambered a shell in his rife.

As he reached the place where Storm and Bear were looking into the forest, Luke saw a brown bear larger than he thought possible. Although the beast came straight at him, Luke held his ground. The bear was about fifteen feet from Luke when it stood up on his rear feet, growled, and swung its right paw with such power that Luke knew a single swipe could kill a man or animal.

As the bear started to move forward, Luke fired his first shot into the large animal's chest where his heart should be. The bear screamed and took a half step back then started forward again.

Morning Star was watching from her hiding place by the water. She saw Luke take the first shot then pause and then as the bear started toward him again he started walking straight at the giant. She knew it was a cousin to the grizzly, close to nine feet tall standing on his back legs. He fired four more shots so fast it sounded like one long sound all hitting the bear in an area no bigger than the diameter of a coffee cup. The bear opened his mouth to growl, but no sound came out, just the blood that was foaming from his lips.

Luke dropped his rifle to the ground, pulled his knife from its sheath, and took two steps into the bear's kill zone. With one very swift move he slit the bear's throat. Luke took three steps backward and crossed his arms. He just stood there still holding his prized possession in his right hand as the giant bear crashed to the ground, dead.

Morning Star came running, screaming at the top of her lungs, "Are you crazy?" The Ute Indians had no swear words in their language, which was lucky for Luke because she was fuming and so upset she was almost in tears.

"You fool, you could have been killed—then what would I do? I just met you, and you are already trying to get away from me. I should take that rifle of yours and smack you in your head to see if your brains are still there!"

Luke looked puzzled and didn't understand what she was so upset about. In his mind it was just another part of his growing and becoming a man and a warrior. They rode back to the village without speaking even though Morning Star wrapped her arms around Luke's waist much tighter than necessary and laid her head against his back. Luke liked the feel of her arms around him, even though he knew she could ride all day without holding on. People of the Horse, he thought to himself.

Chapter 11

They rode into the village, and people just smiled and pointed, in a good way. They both blushed just a little, but they were beginning to feel very comfortable with each other.

That evening after Luke finished telling the story of the bear and telling his cousins they could have the skin if they would go and take it from the bear, he and Morning Star walked through the village and down by the lake, with Storm and Bear following close behind.

Morning Star asked, "Tell me they won't be sleeping with us after we are a couple?"

Luke started to turn a little red in the face; he had definitely thought of that possibility, but he was not sure enough of himself to bring something like that up. Apparently Morning Star did not share the same insecurities.

The next morning Luke planned to go and round up some of the wild horses like the ones his pa always brought back to Taos to sell. He borrowed two lariats and some lengths of braided rawhide lead ropes from his grandfather.

After eating a large breakfast of maize with some boiled meat in it (scrapple) and then fried crisp along with some squaw bread and honey, he called Storm to his side and the three companions rode off to the northwest. He rode for about thirty minutes at a leisurely pace and noticed dust rising from the trail that led back toward the village. Bear barked twice and Luke brought Storm to a stop then waited. A few minutes later Morning Star came riding up at full speed and slid her pinto pony to a stop.

Luke looked concerned and asked, "What's wrong?"

She replied, "You idiot! You forgot something!"

Luke asked in a serious tone, "What?"

"Me, you fool!"

She rode off ahead of him for a few minutes, and Luke realized he had no clue how to act around a woman. Morning Star finally allowed Luke to catch up. She asked, "Well, Mr. Bear Killer, do you have a plan to catch your wild horses, or are you just going to shoot them?" trying to hide the smile on her face.

Luke noticed it and said, "I thought I'd just have you scream at them. That should be enough to make them stop in their tracks long enough so I can get a rope on them."

They giggled and rode on. Luke at last explained his plan to Morning Star as they rode.

"I hope we can find some down by the deep spot in the stream where they drink. I want to run them for a mile or so, and then I'll backtrack to the water hole and hide, while you and Bear slowly turn the herd back to the water so I can get a rope on the one I want."

She was impressed. "You have thought this through, haven't you?" she asked.

"Yeah I have, and I just hope you can keep up!" he exclaimed.

Now her face was turning red, and not with embarrassment. They rode for another mile or so, and the water hole came into view. Luke saw exactly what he was hoping for: horses all around the natural tank, some grazing, some drinking.

Luke said, "OK, this is perfect. You and Bear circle around to the right. I'll go left, and we'll herd them off to the west. When you see me turn back, keep them going for another half a mile or so then head them back toward the tank. I'll be in the reeds on the right side of the water hole."

Morning Star just nodded and started around the back side of the tank.

Luke turned to Bear and said, "Bear, stay with her." The big pup looked up at Luke his tail wagging and barked. Then he took off at a full run after Morning Star's Indian pony.

Luke nudged Storm with his heels, and they headed for the herd. It looked like thirty to forty horses in the herd, and there was a very large palomino that Luke made out to be the leader. The big golden horse rose up on his back legs and whinnied then headed for the west at a fast gallop. The rest of the herd started to run and fall into a bunch behind the lead horse.

Luke looked across the herd and could see Morning Star riding with both hands in the air swinging a lariat and yelling at the herd. Luke thought to himself, "Lord, she sure can sit a horse." He had never seen a woman who could handle a horse the way she did. The reins were lying on her lap, and she was controlling the movements of her pony with only her heels. The horse seemed to know exactly what she wanted. Bear ran alongside her pony, and Luke knew he was smiling.

They rode for a good distance up the valley when Luke noticed that the wild horses were beginning to tire. He turned Storm in a large circle and started back toward the waterhole at a dead run. Morning Star saw Luke turn, and she thought to herself, "Lord, he sure can sit a horse."

Luke made it back to the reeds by the water hole, slid off Storm, and dropped his reins to the ground. The horse started to graze in the lush grass. Luke moved through the reeds and got as close to the water as he could and still stay out of sight. He made himself stealth the way his pa had taught him when they were hunting and fishing. He stayed perfectly still as Morning Star and Bear herded the horses back to the water. Then they broke off to the right and over into the trees so as not to spook the herd.

Luke could see two horses he had noticed as they ran; one was a young paint horse only about six feet away. Luke decided it would be his target. He slowly removed one of the lariats from his shoulder and laid it into his hand. He was totally focused on the paint horse. Slowly, he stood, knowing the herd would spook when they noticed him.

He twirled the lasso once, twice, and then let it fly. The paint horse realized something was wrong and lifted his head just as Luke's lariat hit the horse, keeping the leather rope from going over his head. But the young horse moved to its left, and the rope dropped down around its neck. It was lucky for Luke that there were no other horses between himself and the paint.

Luke stepped out of the reeds already talking to the young horse in a very soft, yet controlling voice, "Easy fella, just stay calm."

The horse had panic in its eyes as the rope started to tighten, but something about the voice coming from the other end seemed to quiet him down and kept him from bucking and trying to run. He did try to back up and get up on his hind legs but Luke kept shortening the distance between the horse and himself. When the young horse stopped rearing and came back down to the ground, Luke was there with the slack out of the rope and talking softly. The horse responded by pawing the ground a few times and then snickered. It was over, Luke had won. Luke and Morning Star moved the young horse over into the trees, about thirty feet back from the meadow, and tied him to a tree where he could graze in the grass.

They repeated the entire process from beginning to end one more time, and Luke found the buckskin horse he wanted, with the same result as with the paint. Morning Star had seen a lot of wild horses caught. Her people were known for their skills with the horse, but never with such little effort. This young man truly has the gift, she thought.

They rode back toward the village. Luke talked to the wild horses and touched them as they rode. He let the lassos fall against the horses till it no longer bothered them, and by the time they reached the village, he was able to do whatever he wished around them. He put the new horses in the large corral the villagers had for gentling and training.

That evening as he and Morning Star walked by the lake, she mostly just stared at him, trying to figure out what made this young man she had feelings for so special. Luke would ask, "What?" She would just smile, say nothing, and squeeze his arm. Luke wasn't sure what to make of it but he didn't want it to end.

Luke worked with his horses every morning, and Morning Star was always close by along with Storm and Bear. By the end of the fifth day Luke had the two horses doing exactly what he wanted. He could work them in a circle in the big corral without a lead rope; he could turn them and have them go in the opposite direction with just a hand gesture. They would gallop and then slide to a stop on command.

Chapter 12

The next morning Morning Star fixed Luke a big breakfast of scrapple, smoked fish, and fresh berries. He was impressed and said to her, "So you're not just a good-looking woman, you can cook and ride and who knows what else?"

"Would you like to find out?" she asked him.

Luke didn't blush as much as he would have a week ago. He said, "Yes, I believe I would."

After they ate, Luke said, "I need to give Storm and Bear some exercise. Would you like to come?"

"Of course."

They rode for a while, and Luke asked, "How far is the fort? I would like to see what kind of supplies they have."

"It's about an hour from here."

They headed in that direction. When they reached the fort, Luke was surprised at how large it was and the number of people who lived inside the log walls. They tied their horses at the hitching post so they could drink, and Bear sat on the boardwalk by the door into the trading post. They walked through the door, and Luke was struck with the enormous amount of dry goods, feed, and guns. There were shotguns, rifles, and many different kinds of handguns.

Morning Star asked him, "Are you good with a pistol?"

He replied, "I'm a very good shot but not so quick on the draw. It just doesn't seem to make sense in my head."

"Is that why you don't carry a pistol?"

"No," he said, "I just haven't had the need to so far."

They had been looking for almost an hour when Luke saw a mattress standing in the corner.

"Morning Star, look at this," he said.

"What is it?"

"A mattress."

"What's it for?" she asked.

"To sleep on!"

"Why?"

"Because I don't like sleeping on the ground, and for your information I don't like being cold, either."

The man behind the counter came over and asked, "Can I help ya, young feller?"

"How much is something like that?" Luke asked.

The clerk said, "Seventeen dollars. Can I load it up fer ya?"

To that, Luke replied, "Wow! I don't have any way to haul it, but as soon as I get back to Taos I'm gonna order me one for sure."

They looked around for a little longer, and then Luke bought them a sarsaparilla. Morning Star smiled and said, "It's been a long time since I've had one of these. I've forgotten how good it is."

"I'm glad you like it," he said.

They walked outside, sat on a bench on the boardwalk, and watched the people moving in all directions going about their daily chores. About that time Luke noticed a very large man riding a horse that looked like it hadn't been eating on a regular basis. The man looked to be a trapper or mountain man. He had a scraggly beard, long hair, and a long rifle across his legs as he rode into the fort. He rode up to the hitchin' post and stepped off the poor animal. Luke noticed the smell coming off the man; it was all Luke could do to keep from gagging.

The man reached out with his right foot and kicked Storm in the flanks to move him over to make room for his horse. Luke jumped to his feet, looked the smelly man straight in the eye, and said, "Mister! Don't be messin' with my horse."

He looked at Luke and asked, "Well, ya little piece of shit, where'd ya get a horse like that?"

Luke replied, "That really ain't any of yer concern, now is it?"

Then the man noticed Morning Star, and he said, "Is that yer squaw, boy? You just seem to have all the luck. I believe I'll just get me some of that."

Luke replied, "Ya better watch yer mouth, mister."

The big man got down from his horse, and you could hear the horse sigh in relief as the weight was gone.

"You wouldn't mind if'n I took yer squaw out back by the stable and had myself a little taste of that, would ya?"

Luke was starting to lose his temper when he remembered what his pa would say in a spot like this: "Don't let yer temper put you in a situation you can't control." The man was about ten feet from Luke when he pulled a skinning knife out of a sheath on his belt. He had it in his right hand, and said to Luke, "I'm gonna have me some of that squaw, but first I think I'll just peel some of yer skin to give ya somthin to think about while I show yer woman what a real man's like."

Luke reached for his knife, and he heard Morning Star say, "You're crazy. You smell like a goat that's been dead for a week and look like you ain't had a bath in a year."

Luke saw fire in the man's eyes as Morning Star's words sunk in. The large man stepped closer and said, "Well, maybe I'll just skin her when I'm through, too."

Luke stepped in front of the man as the man started to make a pass at Luke with his knife. Luke took a step toward the man, turning 45 degrees to his left, and came down with his own knife across the wrist of the man. He screamed, fell to his knees, and just looked at his hand laying on the boardwalk still holding his skinning knife. He looked up at Luke and yelled, "Ya little sumbitch! How the hell am I sposed to hunt and trap with no hand?"

"Should've thought about that before you came at me with yer blade. You made two mistakes: you kicked my horse and you insulted my lady."

The man was in so much pain; he screamed and held his wrist.

"You little sumbitch . . . . When I get patched up I'm coming after yer ass, and I'm gonna kill ya!"

Luke looked at him and said, "That's yer third mistake." Luke stepped forward, and with one quick backhand move cut the big man's throat. He fell to the boardwalk with his left hand to his neck and said no more, ever! He was lying in a pool of his own blood. People had gathered round as the big man was pushing Luke, thinking the young man wouldn't stand up to him. They began to clap, and one old man said, "That sumbitch been askin' fer that fer years, just that he had everyone around here buffaloed."

The commander of the fort walked up shortly after the man hit the ground and asked, "What's yer name, young fella?"

Luke told him, kinda worried about what kind of trouble he might be in.

"I'm Captain Clark," the man said, and reached out his hand to Luke; they shook.

"I saw the whole thing so you don't have a thing to worry about."

Luke thanked the captain, who said, "That's a pretty nice Sharps long rifle layin' there. Looks like it yours. He ain't gonna need it in hell, I'm sure of that."

Luke picked it up and examined it. It looked to be the only thing the trapper had that he took care of. Luke went back inside the trading post and found a canvas cover to fit the rifle, knowing Dark Moon would have a special sheath of the finest deer skin for it by morning. While he was inside he bought some .52 caliber cartridges for the long rifle, and he noticed a pad of heavy paper about twelve by sixteen inches that said sketch pad and Luke purchased that as well.

Luke walked outside, grabbed the reins of the trapper's horse, and walked it over to the livery stable. He asked the old timer running the place if he would feed and care for the horse till it was healthy again and then find it a good home. He pitched the old man a twenty dollar gold piece.

The old man smiled and said, "I'll be happy to. And I know a young fella who'll be right proud to have this bronc. I'll see he takes real good care of it too, and," then the old man said, "Thanks, mister."

Luke and Morning Star climbed on their horses and started back in the direction of the village. Luke had the new long rifle across his lap, and Morning Star was carrying the pad of artist paper. Luke looked around but couldn't see Bear. Then he noticed him coming up the trail from the fort at a run. He had something in his mouth. The pup caught up to them, and Luke slid down from Storm as Bear sat down in front of him and dropped a hand still holding the skinning knife. Luke looked at the pup with amazement.

"Yeah, I guess yer right. It is a pretty nice knife," he said as he patted Bear on the head, then stuck the knife down inside the legging of his left moccasin. He picked up the hand and gave it a toss over into the bushes, thinking to himself that the wolves would find and enjoy it by dark. He jumped back on Storm, and they rode off in the direction of the village.

Luke noticed that Morning Star was being unusually quiet as they rode, and he finally asked what was bothering her. She didn't answer but just looked at him with a strange expression on her face for several seconds, then she asked, "You killed that man, and it didn't bother you?"

Luke thought and then replied, "What bothered me was that he said he was gonna come after me and kill me when he got patched up. He would figure out that he couldn't take me in a fair fight so he would more than likely back shoot me, and I don't want to be looking over my shoulder from now on."

Chapter 13

Luke had been in the village for more than two weeks and was thinking he should be heading for Taos, but he really didn't want to leave Morning Star and his family, the People of the Horse. He decided to stay another week.

He spent his time working with his horses, drawing pictures of the children, the mountains, and, of course, Morning Star, who just like Storm or Bear was never too far away. One time as he was sketching he let the memory of the dead trapper come to mind, and he remembered what his pa had told him as he taught Luke to defend himself: never look for trouble but never run from it. If you do it will just follow you and bite you in the butt. If you have to defend yourself, make sure that person can never come at you again. He never thought of the trapper again.

On the sixth day late in the afternoon, his grandmother Dark Moon came to him and said, "My son, there is trouble in your other village, and you are needed there."

Luke asked how she knew this and was it serious. She just shrugged and said, "I don't know everything, but you should get a good night's rest and leave at sunup."

Luke spent the evening with Morning Star. They ate, walked, sat by the lake, and talked, but she could tell that Luke was distracted. He finally told her what his grandmother had said and asked her if she would care for his horses and long rifle because he would be traveling light and fast. He said he would return for them as soon as he could. She said, "Of course."

The next morning at sunup, Luke had fed Bear and made sure Storm was ready to run. He had his Winchester slung over his right shoulder and his leather pouch with some dried jerky and squaw bread in one section and cartridges for his rifle in the other. He kissed his grandmother, hugged his grandfather, and shook hands with his uncle and cousins. He was just getting ready to jump up on Storm when Morning Star stepped up and planted a big ol' kiss on his mouth. It took him by surprise, but it felt good on his lips, and he responded to her, kissing her in return. He jumped up on Storm, nudged him in the flanks, and they were off. Bear ran right beside Storm and barked and was having the time of his young life.

Luke rode hard for almost an hour and a half, and he was amazed at how much ground they had covered. He reined Storm into the stream to drink, and Bear followed. They were both standing in the water drinking but neither were really thirsty; they were ready to run. Luke could tell that neither of them were winded so he said, "Well, OK then. Let's go!" and they were off again like the wind.

Luke wasn't sure what time of day it was, but he thought it was probably midafternoon. Then, there they were—the rooftops of Taos. Luke couldn't believe they had traveled that far in such a short period of time; it almost seemed impossible, and yet here they were.

Luke headed Storm at a fast gallop down the trail on the east side of town that ran behind the butcher shop and slid him to a stop by the back door. There was no fire in the smoker and that was unusual; things seemed very quiet for this early in the day. Papa Jo always worked much later.

Luke walked into the butcher shop through the back door and called out, "Mama B! Papa! Is anyone here?"

He heard Mama B call out in a very weak voice, "we're in here."

He walked into their sitting room and found her in her favorite chair. Her face was badly bruised and swollen; she had two black eyes, her upper lip was split, and her left arm was in a sling.

She said, "Oh Luke, my son! I'm so glad to see you."

He dropped to his knees and kissed her hand softly, and asked, "How did this happen, and where is papa?"

She motioned to the bedroom, and Luke stood and walked through the door. He saw Papa Jo lying in the bed with bloody bandages around his head and cuts and bruises all over his face. Luke could hear him breathing but just barely, and there was a rattling coming from his chest. He returned to the other room and found Mama B had fallen asleep.

He walked out back and around to the livery stable where he found Gunther trying to work some iron without much success, his right arm in a sling.

"What's goin' on around here?" Luke demanded.

Gunther said, "Oh boy, Luke, I'm so glad yer home. I'll give ya the short version. Two trappers were gettin' some smoked meat from Papa, and they were all liquored up and said they weren't gonna pay him. They started laughin' at him and . . well, ya know how he cusses, and it gets even worse when he gets upset. Well, they started pistol-whippin' him, and they beat him up really bad. When Mama B came out to see what all the racket was, they started on her, and then they shot Skeeter. Lord, Mama B loved that dog. I heard the ruckus and come runnin' over to see if I could help out. When I came through the back door, one of them sumbitches shot me in the shoulder."

Luke started to fume. "Are they still in town?" he asked.

Gunther replied, "Yeah! They're camped about a quarter-of-a-mile north of town in that grassy spot by the stream. They been goin' to the saloon in the afternoon, and since the marshal left for Santa Fe early yesterday before this all happened, they been gittin' all drunk and fightin' with anyone that goes into the saloon. Harry down there is plumb scared; he's afraid they're gonna shoot him if he don't keep servin' 'em. He says they ain't paid him a penny and probably don't intend to."

Luke asked, "Is Miguel next door?"

"Yeah. He stayed here last night; he was afraid to go home."

"Gunther, you just sit down and rest a little and let me handle this."

Luke walked into the gun shop, and Miguel's face lit up.

"Mister Luke, you're home—thank you my God!"

"Miguel, I need a shotgun and some shells."

"I know what you're gonna do. Please, please, be careful!" he pleaded, but he knew Luke's mind was made up.

"Look at these one. Mr. Gunther just traded for eet. Eet's from England or Europe or someplace far away. Eet don't have no hammers, but eet shootses very good."

Luke looked it over, and the barrels were on top of each other instead of side by side. And Miguel was right: no hammers. Luke found the lever to the breech of the gun, and Miguel said, "When you putt the shells in and close eet, eet cocks itself, and that little button by the trigger is the safety. Push it to the right with your thumb and it's on, and to the left with your finger and it's off."

Luke dropped two twenty-gauge shells in the barrels and snapped it shut. He didn't bother to put the safety on. Luke took the shotgun and a half-dozen shells and was starting to leave when Miguel stopped him.

"Mr. Luke! You better take this," Miguel said and handed Luke a beautiful, silver, engraved Colt .45 Peacemaker. "Eets loaded and ready to go. You may not have time to reload the shotgun."

"I don't carry a pistol," Luke said.

"Please! Take eet. Eet's better to have one and not need eet than need one and not have eet."

Luke stuck the Colt into his belt on the left side so it would be out of the way, but he could reach across with his right hand and pull it if he needed it.

He walked outside and Gunther said, "Luke! Please be careful."

Luke just nodded as he headed up the street. Old Hank was pushing his wooden wheelbarrow that had a big square-nosed shovel in it, and he was making his afternoon rounds picking up horse manure, up one side of the street and then back down the other every morning and afternoon just as regular as clock.

Old Hank looked up and said, "Howdy, Luke. How ya doin'?"

But Luke just kinda dipped his head a little to let the old man know he had heard him and kept on walking toward the saloon.

Luke walked through the swinging doors and immediately noticed there were only three people in the small saloon, Harry Vaughn the bar keep and two men standing at the bar. Luke walked up to the bar with the shotgun at his side. He laid the scatter gun on the bar with the barrel pointed at the two men about twenty feet to his left.

"Hey, Luke," Harry said in a voice so soft that Luke almost didn't hear, "what can I get fer ya?"

"Just a beer, Harry."

Luke took a sip of his beer but never took his eyes off of the two men at the bar. He knew they were aware of him, and finally the one closest to him said, "Ain't you a little young to be in a saloon, squirt?" and they both chuckled.

The other one said, "Yeah! Shouldn't ya be suckin' on a tit somewhere? Yer momma's probably lookin' fer ya right now," and they both laughed.

Luke just stared at the men with so much anger in his eyes it was all he could do to stay calm. He spoke directly to the two men.

"Have ya tried some of the meat at the butcher shop yet?"

And the first man said, "Yeah, we were in there yesterday afternoon," a fact that Luke already knew.

"Ya know, when ya take something and don't pay for it, it's called stealing."

The first man denied taking anything but was beginning to realize what Luke was getting at. The men started to get riled, and one said, "Ya don't know what yer talkin 'bout, ya little shit. Ya better go mind yer own affairs before I give ya a taste of this here rifle butt."

Luke asked, "You like hittin' folks with that rifle and those pistols butts?"

The first man scowled and said, "Yeah, I do. And it looks like it's yer turn."

Luke squeezed the front trigger on the shotgun. Fire belched from the barrel and hit the first man in his right knee, blowing it completely away. The blast spun him around 180 degrees, and he fell forward into the arms of the second man who was trying to get his pistol cocked and up in Luke's direction.

The first man was screaming uncontrollably, sliding down the chest of the second man toward the floor while the other man struggled to free his gun. He pulled the trigger and the .45 slug buried into the two-by-twelve wooden-plank floor about three feet away from Luke's feet. Luke slowly pulled the Colt .45 from his belt and in one smooth motion cocked the pistol, pointed, and squeezed the trigger. A .45 slug hit the second man in the forehead just above the bridge of his nose. The back of his head exploded, spewing brain matter, blood, and bone all over the side wall of the saloon. There was a hole about the size of a coffee cup at the back of his head. His knees buckled, and he dropped straight down, sitting on the heels of his old worn boots then he fell backward and looked up at the ceiling, dead and on his way to hell.

The first man was lying on the floor moaning and trying to hold his knee that didn't exist. The bottom of his leg, calf, ankle, and foot were just hanging on by a shred of meat and a small amount of tendon. Luke walked up to him and shot him in the other knee, and he screamed even louder.

"Why are you doin' this . . . are you crazy?" he cried.

Luke looked him straight in the eyes and said, "Yeah, I am a little crazy right now. The old couple in the butcher shop are very close friends of mine, and they might not make it."

"I'm sorry!" the man wailed, "We were drunk. We didn't know what we were doin'. Please stop."

"Sorry about what?" Luke asked. "Sorry that you did it or sorry that you got caught?"

The man didn't answer.

"And the dog you shot! He was very special to me, and here you lay sayin' yer sorry. Ya son of a bitch," Luke said and placed the barrel of the Colt up against his left temple and sent the man straight to whatever is waiting on the other side of life. It didn't matter to Luke what was there or how bad it was; it wasn't bad enough for these two.

He walked over, removed their gun belts, and went through their pockets. Each man had over three hundred dollars. They must have sold some furs or robbed some poor farmers. Luke asked Harry how much the two men owed him, and he replied "About twelve dollars." Luke went over, picked up his drink, and took a long pull on it. Then he counted out a hundred dollars in cash and laid it on the bar. He reached in his pouch and took out a fifty-dollar gold piece and flipped it to Harry. He caught it and said, "This is way too much money."

But Luke said, "You may have to give the undertaker a couple of bucks to cover the funerals. If it were up to me, I'd haul their sorry butts out of town and leave them for the buzzards and coyotes.

"Well! I guess I better walk on over to their camp and check on their stock." Luke said.

Luke walked out the swinging doors and left Harry standing there speechless and shaking his head. Luke heard Miguel coming up from behind calling, "Mr. Luke, are you OK?"

And he said, "I'm fine. Just go on back, and I'll be there as soon as I round up their gear."

At the trappers camp he found the wagon that he had seen on the way into town but paid no attention to. It had some furs, a couple of Winchesters, a new Sharps long rifle, and some other odds and ends. They had a saddle horse down by the stream and two of the finest mules Luke had ever seen. Luke remembered his pa saying one time, "If you ever get a matched pair of mules with good tempers you hang on to them cause they'll work circles around any pair of horses. They're strong, sure-footed, and smart as a whip, and if you can find that combination you will really have a prize."

Luke looked at them for a minute. They were both buckskin color, but one had a black mane and tail and black stockings on its front legs while the other had a palomino color to its main, tail, and front stockings. He walked up to them talking gently and rubbed his hands on their rumps and up their backs as he walked between them. They each turned their head to look at Luke, but neither showed any concern. Luke thought, "That takes care of the temperament."

He started to hitch the one with the black mane to the wagon, and each time he was about ready to put the harness on, the mule would back away from him. Finally, after several tries, he let the mule go where he had a mind to. He walked around and backed up to the wagon on the other side of the tongue, and the one with the golden mane moved right into the other spot on the right. Luke just scratched his head and thought, "That takes care of the smarts." They each had their place and that was that.

Luke tied the horse to the back of the wagon with a lead rope, climbed up in the wagon seat, and snapped the reins just above their rumps. They started pulling together as smooth as butter.

He walked them down to the livery and decided to try something. He dropped the reins, and as they got to the livery doors

Luke yelled, "WHOA, MULES!" And they took one more step and came to a stop in unison.

Gunther said, "That's very impressive. You should get a very nice price for them two."

Luke said, "Oh no, I already have plans for these guys."

He unhitched the mules, put them in the corral, and gave them some good feed and water. He went back to where Storm and Bear were still standing by the back door of the Johansen's butcher shop. Then he walked the big horse down to the water and waded in with Bear right behind.

Luke led them out of the water on the other side and dropped the reins. Storm began to graze. He had Bear come to the shop with him for some food and realized he hadn't eaten anything all day, either. Luke went into the smokehouse, carved a big pile of beef, and he and Bear sat down by the stream and ate until they were both full. He walked back into the shop and saw that Mama B was still sleeping, although it was a restless sleep, and she moaned a lot. Luke was very worried about her. He walked into Papa Jo's room. His breathing was very shallow, and he could hear the rattle in his chest. He had seen enough death to know what that meant.

Chapter 14

The next morning Luke was up a few minutes before daybreak. He butchered a cow and put the chalkboard out with the day's fare: "Fresh beef." About two in the afternoon he started a fire in the smoker so it would be ready. He had no idea how many customers would come in.

As it turned out, he couldn't keep up with the business. He ended up writing down most of the orders because he couldn't fill them fast enough. He hired Gunther's son Hans to hook up the ox cart to one of the mules and start making the deliveries. As he was finishing cleaning, Hans returned from the deliveries. He had made over four dollars in tips and told Luke he was available any time and would just work for tips. Luke flipped him a five-dollar gold piece, and Hans's eyes got as big as saucers.

Luke went down to the stream and stripped down to his long johns and sat down in the water, letting it run over his aching body. It had been a very long day. He fed Bear and ate a few bites himself, but he was too exhausted to even be hungry. Luke knew that tomorrow would be the same thing all over again. He didn't know why anyone would do this for a living.

He went to his room, laid on his bed roll, and fell asleep almost immediately. He woke with a start in the middle of the night, slipped on his pants and boots, and ran to the butcher shop. Mama B was sleeping in her chair so he quietly looked in on Papa Jo and found he was not breathing. He had passed on not long before Luke had come in to check, he was still at a normal temperature. Luke took his hand and sat in a chair by his side for several hours. He had never regained consciousness since the beating.

They held the funeral the next day. Nearly everyone from the Pueblo de Taos was in attendance, business people, Indians, Mexicans, children, ranchers, and farmers. Papa Jo had helped almost everyone in the area at one time or another. Everyone attended except for Mama B. Her condition had become worse, and she was going downhill rapidly. Gunther's wife stayed with her for the next few days, but three days after the funeral she died. Luke thought she had no reason to live without Papa Jo. He was the only man she had ever known or loved, and he was her best friend.

The next morning at dawn Luke sat by the stream with a cup of hot coffee and Bear at his side. Storm was just across the stream grazing on the sweet green grass. Luke was trying to figure what he should do. He had money but wasn't sure where he should go. He truly loved this valley.

He decided to go see the banker and find out exactly what his financial situation was—maybe that would help him decide on a plan. He would not open the shop until after he returned from the bank. When he walked in the bank at exactly 8:00 a.m. Mr. Weathers the owner and manager met him at the door and shook his hand, telling him again how sorry he was for Luke's loss. He led Luke into his private office, had the clerk bring two cups of hot coffee, then he asked Luke how he could be of service to him. Luke told him he was thinking of drawing his money out and maybe heading back to the people of his father but he really wasn't sure where he would go.

Weathers got a very strange and puzzled look on his face and said, "Luke! I don't understand why would you leave."

Then Luke was puzzled himself and said, "But I have no place here to stay, and I'm sure whoever holds the note on the shop will want to sell it. I have no interest in being a butcher for the rest of my life."

Mr. Weathers just smiled and said, "I guess Papa Jo didn't have a chance to tell you, but while you were gone he and Mama

B put everything in your name. They had no other family and considered you their son."

Luke couldn't quite comprehend at first. He sipped his coffee and tried to get his head around what this meant as he fought back a tear. They talked for a moment and then Mr. Weathers took a ledger out of a locked drawer in his desk and began to list all of the holdings that now belonged to Luke. Five buildings, including the barber and bath house, the general mercantile, and the saloon in the next block up; the 10,500 acres out back halfway up the mountain and all the timber on it. Luke couldn't believe what he was hearing. Weathers went on. Papa Jo and Mrs. Johansen had an account with $42,500.83.

Luke couldn't believe any of this. He asked Mr. Weathers how much the payments on all of this would come to. The banker shook his head and smiled.

"You really don't understand, do ya? There are no payments. You own everything free and clear. Papa Jo never financed anything; he always paid cash as he went. If he needed something and couldn't afford it, he would wait until he had the money before he got it. He cost me a lot of money in interest over the last thirty years, but he was a good friend, and he helped lots of people around this valley. He'll be missed around here, that's for sure."

Luke asked him if he would handle all the paperwork and to move the cash to his account.

"By the way, how much do I have in my account?" asked Luke.

The banker did some figuring in his ledger book, then looked up at Luke and said, "You now have $51,501.00 in cash in your account."

Luke almost choked on the swallow of coffee he had in his mouth. His eyes started to water, and a little coffee tried to come out of his mouth, but he stopped it by covering his mouth with a hand.

"How did it get from forty-two to over fifty-one thousand?" Luke asked.

"Every time Papa Jo made a deposit in his account, he made a deposit in yours as well."

Luke said, "I need to go and try to understand all of this."

Mr. Weathers said, "Go and relax for a while. I'll send the clerk for you this afternoon when I have all the papers ready for you to sign so everything will be official."

Luke thanked him, shook his hand, and had started to leave when he stopped, turned to the bank manager, and said, "Would you do me a favor as your first official act as my banker?"

"Of course, what is it?"

"I would like you to take the deed to the property that the livery and gun shop sit on. Transfer it to Gunther's name and mark it paid in full."

"How much are you going to sell it for?" asked the banker.

Luke pondered this for a few seconds and then said, "Make it one dollar."

He turned, walked out of the bank, and headed back toward the shop. The banker just stood there scratching his head and with a very large grin on his face. He thought to himself, "What a kid."

Luke walked right down the middle of the street still trying to figure out what had just happened.

"Forty-five minutes ago I didn't know where I was going to sleep tonight, and now I'm one of the richest people in town," he said to himself.

In fact he was the richest person in the valley.

Chapter 15

Luke worked the butcher shop from sunup to sundown every day for about three months. He bought livestock from the ranchers and farmers, and business was good, but he wasn't doing what he had planned for his life. He kept trying to find someone to help in the shop but all he could come up with was young Hans, a nice boy but not ready for a full-time position. So Luke butchered and smoked meat, and Hans made the deliveries day in and day out.

This went on for over four months and Luke was beginning to feel like he might be trapped in this butcher shop madness forever. One afternoon around two Luke heard Bear bark a couple of times to make Luke aware that something was going on that he didn't understand. Luke walked out back and saw a buckboard with a man and a woman sitting just looking around. Luke approached the wagon and asked the man if there was something he could do to assist them. The young man who seemed to be in his early twenties jumped down, shook Luke's hand, and said, "I'm Teddy Moore and this is my wife Becky."

Luke asked, "Where y'all headed?"

Teddy said that he had been working for Becky's father on his ranch, the T/ T, between Albuquerque and Santa Fe, but when he found out they were going to get married, he fired him and disowned Becky.

"We left with just what ya see in the wagon and the clothes on our backs."

Luke said, "I know how that can happen. Why don't ya pull yer wagon off the trail up close to the stream and unhitch yer horse? You can hobble him on the other side of the stream and let him graze. Why don't y'all get some rest and cleanup, and come up to the store in a couple of hours and we'll have some dinner."

Teddy and Becky just stared at each other; they had been on the trail for three-and-a-half days, and no one had offered them a hand of any kind.

Luke fixed smoked ham, some boiled potatoes, and squaw bread with some fresh apples for dessert. The Moores ate like they were starving, and Luke thoroughly enjoyed their company.

Teddy said to Luke, "This sure is a fine butcher shop you have here. Is it yours?"

Luke replied, "Aah . . . Yeah, I guess it is," and he asked Teddy, "Do you know anything about butcherin'?" knowing it would be too good to be true.

Teddy said, "Well, as a matter a fact I do. I started out as a cowhand at the T/T and then Mr. Trout decided he wanted me to help out the cook 'cause he had thirty-five hungry cowboys to feed three times a day, and his helper got his self shot in a poker game over Albuquerque way. The old cook at the ranch was really something, and I guess he took a likin' to me 'cause he went out of his way to show me how to skin and butcher all the different animals, and how to get the prime cuts and what to do with all the innards, and how to tan the skins. And I turned out to be a pretty good cook, too. Not as good as Becky 'cause she had some real trainin' at one of them fancy restaurants back in New York City, but still pretty dang good."

Luke was about to bust his buttons. He was tryin' not to show any excitement, but his insides were churnin' and he was figurin' how he could hang on to this young couple. Luke finally just came out and asked (he didn't know how else to broach the subject), "Where ya headed?"

They just looked at each other and shrugged.

"We're really not sure. We decided to just take off and see where the trail led us."

Luke was smiling inside.

"How long since y'all have slept in a real bed?"

"It's been a while for me," Becky said, and Teddy added, "I ain't never laid my head on a store-bought bed that I know of."

Luke stood up, asked them to follow him, led them into the Johansen's bedroom. The young couple just looked around in amazement. Luke said, "Why don't you spend the night here? It's always easier to make a decision after you've had some rest."

Becky said, "Isn't this your parents' room?"

Luke replied, "It was, but they're both dead. And besides, I know they would like to see you enjoy it. They were very special people."

Luke went out back to his room but had trouble falling asleep as he thought of being able to get back to the outdoors once again. He finally fell asleep thinking of Morning Star and the two of them riding along some babbling brook.

Chapter 16

The Moores woke to the smell of fresh coffee. They dressed quickly and walked out of the bedroom to find Luke sitting at the table feeding Bear some scraps of meat. Becky gasped and said, "Oh my! Is that a bear?"

Luke smiled and said, "Naw! Just a pup."

"That's the biggest dog I've ever seen, replied Becky. "Is he friendly?"

"I sure hope so, or we're all in a heap of trouble," replied Teddy.

Becky said, "You two just sit and relax while I rustle up some breakfast."

"You don't have to cook fer me," Luke assured her.

But Teddy said, "Let her cook. Yer in for one heck of a treat, I promise."

"How'd y'all sleep?" Luke asked.

Teddy smiled, and Becky's eyes rolled back in her head a bit.

"That bed was heaven," she said, and Teddy added, "I ain't never slept on anything like that before."

Luke asked, "How would you like to sleep on it every night?"

Teddy wasn't sure he had heard him right and asked, "What do ya mean?"

Luke asked, "You're a butcher, right?" Teddy shook his head to affirm. "And this is a butcher shop. I need some help if yer interested."

Teddy asked, "Are you serious? Just yesterday we was wonderin' what we were gonna do and now yer offerin' me a job? That's amazing."

"Well, I was thinking last night that I really need someone around here so I can take care of some of my other chores, and there'll be plenty of work for Becky, too. So what do ya think?" asked Luke.

Teddy almost choked on a mouth full of coffee.

"Hell, yes! . . . I mean, I'd be proud to work for ya, and I guarantee you won't have to look over yer shoulder, neither," Teddy said.

Becky served up some ham and scrambled eggs with onion and tomatoes in them and some kind of seasoning Luke had never tasted before, fried potatoes with some peppers and onions, and hot biscuits. Teddy was right, Luke had never tasted a breakfast like this. What a treat. Luke told them that the sitting room with the fireplace, the bedroom, and the kitchen were all theirs, and Becky broke down and cried like a baby or a new bride, Luke wasn't sure which.

They all smiled and had another cup of coffee. Becky couldn't keep the tears from running down her pretty young face. Teddy stood and said, "Well, hell! I guess we better get to work."

Luke said, "Hey! Just hold on a minute," and Teddy gave him a look of apprehension.

"Is something wrong?" he asked.

Luke said, "Sit back down and have another cup while we hammer out some details."

"Like what?" Teddy asked.

"Well, don't you want to know how much yer gonna be paid?" asked Luke.

Teddy asked with a smile, "You mean yer gonna let us sleep in that bed, live in this beautiful house, eat fresh meat, and yer gonna pay me, too?"

"Ya, well! I was thinkin' twenty-five dollars to start," Luke said.

"All this and twenty-five dollars a month besides. That's great," Teddy said.

Luke said, "Ah no, I meant twenty-five dollars a week—each!"

This time Teddy did spit his coffee down the front of his shirt, and Becky took a deep breath and held it. "This must be a dream," she thought to herself.

Teddy said, "Are you crazy? That's two hundred dollars a month!" Then he said, "I meant 'serious,' ah, not 'crazy,' Mr. Kash."

Luke said, "I'm very serious, and call me Luke. Mr. Kash was my pa and he's dead."

Luke and Teddy butchered a cow, and Luke found Teddy to be a very skillful butcher. As he cut different pieces of meat from the hanging carcass, he would tell Luke what they were called, what was the best for steaks and stew and roasts. He showed Luke some parts that should go directly to the smoker 'cause they were so tough they would need to smoke for ten to twelve hours but then be as tender as a baby's bottom.

"You'll be able to cut it with a fork," Teddy explained.

Luke was somewhat skeptical, but he couldn't deny the man's ability. They worked all day and into the early evening with very little rest, and as the sunset was disappearing Becky came out and informed them that dinner was almost ready.

Luke and Teddy walked down to the stream, washed, and made small talk as they prepared themselves for whatever Becky had been cooking that smelled so good. They ate steak and mashed potatoes and some sliced tomatoes with some kind of sauce on them and life was good!

Luke finished his meal and felt like he would burst. He leaned back in his chair and said, "Miss Becky, that may have been the very best meal I have ever had. What kind of steak was that exactly?" She replied that in the fancier restaurants in New York they call them Filet Mignon, and they are the best part of the cow and very expensive.

Luke said, "That's for sure, and I just added another paragraph to our agreement."

"What?" she asked, knowing this was all too good to be true.

Luke said, "Whenever I'm in town you have to cook for me."

Becky smiled and asked, "Is that all?"

"Absolutely!" Luke replied. Then she put a piece of apricot pie in front of the two men and Luke finally said, "I surrender, I quit, no mas, no mas!"

Everyone laughed and had some coffee with some secret spices that Becky refused to divulge the origin of. She said jokingly, "Excuse me, sir, but I can't go giving all my secrets away! Why, I don't even know you." They all laughed some more and then turned in for the night.

A few days later Gunther approached Luke needing to talk. They went into the butcher shop, and Becky served hot coffee and some fresh pastry. Gunther asked Luke if it would be all right if he were to add another room onto the small living quarters at the rear of the livery. He said he had saved a few dollars and they could use the room. He had discussed it with Papa Jo just before the problem at the shop and hadn't got an answer. Luke jumped up and said, "I'll be right back." He returned with his pouch and handed Gunther an envelope. Gunther asked, "What is this?"

Luke replied, "A man doesn't need to ask to make changes to his own property."

"I don't understand," said Gunther and gave Luke a strange look.

Luke asked "How long have you been renting that space from Papa Jo?"

Gunther replied, "Goin' on twenty years now."

Luke said, "You should be able to save a bit more now that you don't have any rent payments. I meant to give you this a while back but with all the goins-on it plumb slipped my mind."

Gunther opened the envelope, took out a deed that listed him as owner, and it was paid.

"I think Papa would have wanted you to have this."

Tears came to Gunther's eyes. He hugged Luke, thanked him, and said, "I never expected to own anything. I could never save enough money to think about it."

Luke asked, "Can we still be partners in buyin' and sellin' guns?" and Gunther smiled and said, "of course."

Luke said, "I need to talk to Miguel. Is he working in the shop?"

Gunther said, "Yes, he will be happy to see you, he really looks forward to visiting you."

They finished their coffee and walked together back to the livery. Luke went into the gun and leather shop to see Miguel. He beamed when he saw the young man. Luke thought he had never known a happier person.

Luke said, "Tell me about the shells that you gave me for the shotgun I used at the saloon."

Miguel smiled and said, "Oh, Mr. Luke, they are very special. I load them myself. They have pieces of lead instead of buckshot, eight pieces in each shell and extra powder. It's like being hit with eight bullets at once."

Luke thought for a moment.

"Do you still have that shotgun I used?"

"Of course, Mr. Luke."

"Can you cut it down? I don't much care for pistols," Luke said.

"Are you not a good shot?" Miguel asked.

Luke said, "Actually I'm a very good shot, I'm just not comfortable drawing a pistol."

Miguel said, "But you need a pistol, señor. I have an idea. Give me two days and then come back."

Luke walked out the door and stopped to talk to Gunther about an idea that had been bouncin' around in his head for a while.

They talked for several minutes and then Luke said, "Let me get the drawing I've been workin' on."

He returned a few minutes later with several sketches of a wagon with wooden sides and a solid roof. It was longer and wider than a covered wagon and looked more like a cabin than a wagon. Luke continued to explain what he wanted, and Gunther was thinking of ways to brace the sides and add springs to make it ride smoother. Luke could see he was getting excited about the project.

Luke said, "I thought we could use the wagon I got from the two trappers. It's in really good shape and the frame is heavier than most."

They started that afternoon stripping the wagon down to the frame. Gunther had made drawings of the changes he wanted to make, new wheels that were wider and easier to pull, and new springs that would take the pressure off of the axles and have less chance of breaking. Plus, he had an idea about new springs under the seat that would allow Luke to ride longer without that terrible pain in his back that comes from bouncing on a wooden seat all day.

Luke could hear Gunther working late at night making hinges and springs and brackets and braces, and he could see his wagon coming together in his mind. He imagined being out in the mountains hunting and fishing and yet having a nice warm bed up off the ground and a place to eat when the weather was bad.

Luke and Gunther worked on the wagon every day, and Luke was impressed with all the different ideas Gunther came up with. He put a secret compartment under the seat and floorboard so Luke could keep his cash and gold and no one would ever find them. He put a trap door with a rope pull on it in the floor in the middle of the wagon so he and Bear could sneak in or out if they were under attack, along with a latch so they could lock it from the inside. His bed was on hinges and attached to the side of the wall so that it could be folded up to allow Luke more room. Every joint was filled with oakum and then covered with pine tar to make a water and windproof seal.

Luke ordered a mattress like the one he had seen at the fort in Colorado from the general mercantile. Gunther made cabinets along the bottom of the inside wall where Luke could put rifles and shotguns and compartments to hold boxes of ammunition. There was a large locker across the front of the wagon inside the door and behind the front seat for Luke's cooking gear and provisions and room for his extra set of clothes and boots. Luke thought that everything he could think of was built into his cabin.

One afternoon as he was putting the finishing touches on the wagon Gunther came over carrying a miniature stove. He had made it to fit in the very rear corner of the wagon. It was a small pot belly stove for heat, but it had a flat iron plate on top about eight inches deep and twelve inches wide, just large enough to hold a small coffee pot and a frying pan or pot.

Gunther decided he needed a back door and quickly made the hinges so the door would swing out instead of in for more security.

Luke had been so busy with his wagon that he had completely forgotten about Miguel. One morning he saw him standing and looking at him with his hands in the air implying, "Did you forget me?"

Luke apologized to Miguel and walked with him back to his shop.

Miguel handed him a gun belt. On its right side and in front of the sheath for his knife was an odd-looking holster. On the left side was a holster over where his hip would be. It was angled toward the front at about 30 degrees so the butt of a pistol would fit his hand when he reached across for it. There were slots for six shotgun shells on the right side and room for twelve .45 caliber bullets on the left.

Luke unbuckled his belt and tried the new one on; it fit perfectly.

Then Miguel slid the cut-down, over-and-under shotgun into the holster, and Luke realized it was completely different than any holster he had ever seen. Miguel said, "Put your hand on the butt of the gun, señor."

Luke rested his hand on the cut-down stock.

"Now push down on it," Miguel said.

As he did so, the front of the shotgun began to rise; the holster was on a swivel. Luke was totally impressed.

"That's amazing," Luke said and tried it several times until he began to feel the advantage this rig offered.

Miguel picked up his old belt, removed Luke's knife from it, handed it to him, and he placed it in the new sheath. It fit perfectly. Then Miguel handed him the silver-etched Colt .45 Peacemaker and Luke said something looks different.

Miguel smiled and said, "I removed the front and rear sights. When you are shooting in close you will never use them, and they will drag on yer holster and slow you down."

Luke had to admit that the rig had everything he could want. As he thanked Miguel for the gifts and started to walk away. Miguel handed him a wooden box.

"There is ten boxes of shotgun shells and six boxes of .45s. You should practice with the shotgun to know what it will do. I will load you some more shells before you run out."

Luke thanked him again and left to load the ammo in his wagon.

Luke slept in his new cabin that night. He had a buffalo robe draped over the mattress, two heavy wool blankets, and a pillow that was stuffed with goose down. Bear slept on a bear skin rug on the floor, and it was the best night's sleep either of them had ever had.

Chapter 17

Luke and Bear both woke a few minutes before dawn and knew there was something strange outside. When Luke looked out of his wagon, he could just make out some shadows in the meadow across the stream.

He dressed quickly, jumped down, and started walking in that direction. As Luke reached the bridge he recognized his cousins Grey Wolf and White Horse standing by their horses and watching Luke.

"What a surprise! What brings you to this neck of the woods?" he asked as he got close. Luke looked all around, searching for Morning Star and hoping she had come with them.

"Your grandmother said we should come," said Grey Wolf.

Luke stared at them in confusion.

"There's no problem here. Why would she send you?"

They smiled and pointed toward his wagon where Morning Star was standing with her pony and the two horses that Luke had caught and trained.

Grey Wolf said, "She was coming and no one could stop her so Dark Moon said we should ride with her. So here we are."

Luke walked down to where Morning Star was standing with a great smile on her face. They embraced and kissed for over a minute, and Luke was floating on a cloud.

After they put their horses in the corral, fed, and watered them, Luke took them into the shop and introduced them to Becky and Teddy. They all drank hot coffee while Becky and Morning Star prepared a large breakfast of ham, eggs, flapjacks, and Becky's special pastries. They ate and visited for over an hour and then the cousins said they needed to leave for home. After they all said their goodbyes, they mounted up and headed north up the trail behind town.

Luke and Morning Star watched until they were out of sight. As they walked back toward the shop, Morning Star pointed to his wagon. Luke noticed a large pouch on the wagon seat containing his new set of clothes and boots that he left behind in the village. There was also a sheath made of very soft deerskin decorated with turquoise and beads. It contained his long rifle that he had taken from the trapper at the fort. His artist pad was there as well, and he noticed three pouches each about the size of a gourd. Luke had no idea what might be in them. He picked one up and it was very heavy, maybe twenty pounds. He couldn't imagine what was inside. When he looked at Morning Star, she said, "A gift from your grandfather." Luke opened one of the pouches and couldn't believe his eyes—there was GOLD, lots of gold. He just smiled.

Luke had been so busy since he returned from the village, that he hadn't even thought about his possessions.

Later that morning he walked with Morning Star over to the livery to introduce her to Gunther and Miguel. They were both truly happy to meet her and made her feel welcome. He showed the new horses to Gunther and asked him to find a buyer for them. Luke handed Miguel the sheath that contained the long rifle and asked him to check it out and make sure it was in good working condition.

He showed Morning Star the wagon, which she called his lodge. She noticed he had accumulated some more hardware since she had last seen him.

"Do you really need all those guns?" she asked.

He told her, "They all have their purpose."

He pointed out the smoker and smokehouse and showed her the team of mules he had acquired to pull his lodge.

After he finished showing her the immediate area, they mounted their horses and road for hours all over his property.

Bear was happy to see her and even happier to be out and about after staying around the meadow for the last several months. They picked apples from the orchard high up on the mountain and sat by the waterfall that fed the stream down below. It was almost three o'clock when they rode back to the butcher shop. They stabled their horses, and Luke showed her his shack where she could rest and change into some clean clothes. He was sure she didn't have a change but he would take care of that. About an hour later she was walking around the corral and talking to the mules and the horses when Luke came out the back door of the shop.

"Did you get some rest?" he asked.

"No, I'm fine. I was in the cold water and it was very refreshing."

Luke took her by the hand, and they walked north on the trail to the back of the general mercantile and he led her in. He introduced her to the owner, Buck Jones, and his wife Mary.

Buck said, "It's good to see ya, Luke. Ain't seen ya much since ya been back."

I been kinda busy, but hopefully things will get better now that Teddy and Becky are runnin' the shop."

Buck said, "Yeah! What a nice couple. They are really interested in makin' a go of that place."

Mary Jones came up and introduced herself to Morning Star.

"What a beautiful girl," she said, and Morning Star blushed a little and said thank you.

Luke said to Mary, "We're going out to dinner this evening, and she will need a dress and whatever else gals require. She'll also need some everyday duds, so if you'll just fix her up with whatever she needs I'd be much obliged."

Luke said he had some other things that required his attention and that he would meet her back at the shop. She could visit with Becky if she got back before he did.

They went right to work picking out her new wardrobe. Luke turned and walked out the front door. A few minutes later he walked into the bank and caught Mr. Weather's attention. He tried to take a couple of the bags from Luke and almost dropped them when he discovered how heavy they were.

"Oh my! What have we here?" The banker inquired.

"Just a little gift from my father's people," Luke replied. "And I'd be really pleased if you keep this between you and me."

The banker said he understood and wouldn't say a word as far as where it came from. He would have it assayed, he continued, and let him know what it was worth. He told Luke gold was worth nineteen dollars an ounce at this time, two hundred and twenty-eight dollars a pound.

"No matter what, young man, you have a very large amount of money here," he assured him.

Luke told him to take out a fair amount for his trouble and to have it assayed and deposit the rest in his account. After the banking expenses the total came to an even sixty pounds: $17,280.

Luke left the bank and headed across the muddy street by the saloon. He heard laughing and cussing and loud talking coming from inside the saloon, but he didn't bother to look inside. He had just passed the swinging door a couple of steps when he heard what sounded like a gunshot by his right ear. He turned to see a very large man with a bull whip and a big grin on his bearded face.

Luke said, "Mister! I can't see how that was an accident, so what the hell are you doin'?"

The big man smiled, showing his yellow teeth and tobacco-stained lips and mustache.

"You that Kash kid, aintcha?"

Luke said, "Yeah, I am, but that's no reason to be tryin' to take my ear off with that bull whip."

"My name's Bull Mullins, and there's a man up Denver way payin' me four thousand dollars to bring your sorry ass to him dead."

"And why is he so concerned about my ass?" asked Luke.

"You killed a trapper at the fort up in Colorado eight or nine months ago, right?"

Luke said, "Yeah! He came at me with a skinnin' knife, sayin' he's gonna kill me and then take my lady out behind the barn and then skin us both when he was through. He didn't give me any choice."

"That don't mean squat to me," said the big man. "I got two thousand dollars in my pocket, and I'm gonna have two thousand more when I deliver you to Denver."

"You mean you got two thousand dollars with ya?" Luke asked with a smile.

"Yeah, why?"

'Cause it's nice to know that I'm makin' some money for puttin' up with your crap."

"You ain't gonna get a plug nickel 'cause I'm gonna peel some skin off ya with this here bull whip, then I'm gonna kill ya!" and he reared back to take another swipe at Luke with the whip.

Luke took a step forward and caught the whip up high in his left hand about three feet from the end. The whip didn't crack but wrapped around his arm, and as it did the end of the whip brushed Luke's face. He could tell there was blood running down his cheek. He looked at the end of the whip and noticed a horseshoe nail had been braided into the leather end. He took another wrap around his left arm as he stepped closer to keep the whip taut between them and to make sure the big man couldn't get his hand out of the wrist strap. Each time he would try to go for his pistol Luke would take another wrap around his left forearm.

When Luke was about four feet from the big man, Luke said, "Well, Mr. Bull! You really ain't very smart for a man killer, are ya?"

Bull looked at Luke with squinty eyes and said, "What the hell do ya mean, squirt? I am gonna kill ya!"

"Bringin' a bull whip to a gunfight seems a little stupid to me."

"Whatcha mean a gunfight?" he asked.

Luke reached under his buckskin jacket and grabbed his Colt .45 out of his cross-draw holster, and with one smooth movement put a slug in the big man's right knee. He went down screaming in pain, spit coming from his mouth as he tried to speak.

"They say you only carry that big ol' knife!"

Luke replied, "Yeah, well, things change. You wanna tell me the name of the lunatic in Denver that's put money on my head?" Luke asked.

"Why the hell should I?" said Bull.

"'Cause I'm gonna take out your other knee real quick if ya don't."

"Screw ya, ya little snot nose prick!"

"Wrong answer," replied Luke as he pulled the hammer back and took out Bull's left knee. He screamed even louder.

"OH, you sunsabitch! You better kill me 'cause if you don't I'll be comin' after you that's fer sure!"

"Don't worry, I'm gonna kill ya. It's just a matter of whether ya want to lay here in the street and bleed out or ya want to go fast," said Luke. "Now! What's his name?"

"Why do you want to know," asked Bull.

"'Cause I intend to send him a telegraph to let him know I got his money, and if he sends anyone else after me when I get through with the next man, I'll be comin' to Denver for him," and Luke put another .45 slug in the big man's right ankle. He screamed even louder now.

"Alright! Alright! Jesus! Stop shootin me, ya bastard! His name is John Marsh, general delivery, Denver, Colorado."

Luke said, "You wouldn't lie to me, would ya?"

"Why would I?" asked Bull. "Ya already got me bleedin' all over the street."

"'Cause yer not very smart," said Luke. "You've proved that a time or two in the last few minutes." He lifted his Peacemaker and put a .45 caliber slug in Bull's forehead an inch above the bridge of his nose. By this time almost everyone in the south end of town had come out of the saloon and the other businesses around to see what the shots were all about.

The US Marshal Brady Sims had his office in Taos, and he had been standing outside on the boardwalk rolling a smoke when the whole mess started. By the time he realized what was goin' down, Luke already had everything under control.

Marshal Sims walked up to Luke and said, "Well, I guess you took care of that!"

"Yeah, he came at me from behind."

The marshal said, "I know. I saw the whole thing. Do ya know who he was?"

"He said his name was Bull Mullins, and some rich business-man from Denver was payin' him four thousand dollars to bring me back dead," said Luke as he walked over and went through the dead man's pockets. He found twenty-three hundred dollars in cash and another sixty dollars in ten-dollar gold coins.

The marshal said, "That ain't the half of it. I got paper on him, and he's wanted down 'round Albuquerque fer killin' a banker and then shootin' a US marshal as he rode out of town. He's got a thousand dollars on his head, and there's a whole bunch of US marshals that are gonna be beholden to ya."

Luke said, "Well it looks like I've had a pretty profitable day. Can I buy ya a drink, marshal?"

Sims smiled and said, "Yeah! I guess it's about that time, ain't it? And we need to talk."

As they were walking to the saloon, Morning Star came running up with her arms full of packages and a concerned look on her face.

"How did I know it was you? Are you OK," she asked.

"I'm just fine," he said.

"But you're bleeding."

Luke put his hand to his cheek and remembered the nail in the end of the whip.

"I'll be fine. I'm gonna have a quick beer with the marshal, and then I'll see you at the shop. Will ya holler at Gunther to come collect this feller's guns and rig? I guess his horse is already in the livery."

She wandered on down to the butcher shop but didn't have to holler at Gunther. He and Miguel had heard the ruckus and were on their way up the street.

They passed Morning Star, and she just shook her head and asked Gunther, "Does he always find trouble?"

"He seems to be pretty good at it lately," he answered.

The marshal told Luke that he'd get his money for him the next day.

Luke gave him a fifty-dollar gold piece and said, "Have dinner on me, marshal."

Sims said, "That'll buy an awful lot of dinners."

They were drinking and talking when Doc Burns walked in. He took one look at Luke and said, "Let me grab my bag out of my buggy." He tried to give Luke some kind of ugly brown smelly stuff for the pain but Luke said just go on and sew it up. Doc said it looked like six or seven stitches should do it.

Luke said, "Hurry it up, Doc. I gotta go to dinner with a very purdy lady."

Luke tossed Doc Burns a fifty-dollar gold piece. He grabbed it out of the air and almost choked on his shot of whisky when he saw what it was.

"Luke," he said, "that's enough money for me to take both yer legs off and sew 'em back on again!"

Luke said, "You just keep it 'cause it's startin' to look like we're gonna be real good friends, too."

Luke finished his beer and told the marshal, "Well, ya better have a couple of drinks on me, too, and don't waste my money on the rotgut. Drink the good stuff. And if you run out let me know." Then he tossed Harry Vaughn the bartender a fifty-dollar gold piece.

"Thank you, my young friend," said the marshal as Luke walked out the door, and Luke thought to himself, "Friend? A man can't have enough US marshals as friends, and a doctor or two wouldn't hurt, either."

That evening Morning Star was dressed in a new navy blue and white polka dot dress that accented her very trim and beautiful figure and some shoes she hadn't quite mastered walking in but she was giving it her all. Luke had gone down to the stream and bathed and put on his new clothes that just came back from the village. He met her inside of Becky's home, and she was even more beautiful than Luke could imagine.

They crossed the street and walked up to Marcy's diner that was about a block away. Marcy was a middle-aged women, a widow who had started the diner after her husband had been killed by Indians while on a hunting trip about four or five years earlier. She had been the best cook in town until Becky showed up and now it was a draw. Luke was smart enough not to bring the subject up. He had stopped by earlier to tell Miss Marcy they would be coming.

They sat at a table in the corner with a red and white plaid tablecloth and matching napkins and nice silverware. Morning Star looked at Luke, and he looked back and shrugged. Neither one had much knowledge of social skills.

Marcy brought some wine, and Luke asked her if she would join them at least long enough to teach them some table manners. She sat, poured the red wine, and explained the difference between red and white, then she showed them the reason for the different forks and spoons and bread dishes and soup bowls and where to place their napkins. Luke and Morning Star learned together and enjoyed every minute of it.

Marcy snuck off to the kitchen and soon she returned with two bowls of bean soup with ham and some carrots in it. The diners tried their new skills with spoons and giggled at each other. Luke poured more wine.

Marcy cleared the soup bowls away and served the main course: oven-roasted chicken with fresh carrots and mashed potatoes with a wonderful cream gravy. Luke wasn't sure why but this seemed like the best meal he had ever eaten and Morning Star felt the same. By the time they were halfway through, they were beginning to feel very comfortable with the utensils and not self-conscious at all.

Marcy brought a basket of fresh yeast rolls hot out of the oven, and Luke and the lady ate with great abandon, streams of fresh butter dripping down their chins. Luke poured more red wine. After the main course Marcy brought hot coffee and two large pieces of warm apple pie and some heavy cream to pour over it. Luke was beginning to have his doubts about Becky being a contender. They sat and talked till almost nine in the evening.

Marcy had to finally ask them to leave; she had been on her feet since breakfast.

Luke apologized and gave her a twenty-dollar gold coin but then thought better of it and added a ten–dollar gold coin on top of it. He asked if it was enough.

Marcy smiled and said that it was enough for dinners every night for the next two weeks.

It made Luke feel good to see her smile, and it was more money than she had made in the last two days.

They walked back down the street until they were across from the butcher shop. They crossed the street and walked down between the barber shop and the butcher shop to the trail and then down to the stream. They had been sitting there for a few minutes gazing at the stars when Bear came up from behind and startled them.

He rolled in the grass beside them so they could rub his belly. They decided it was time for bed since Bear didn't seem to want to leave them alone. They walked back to the area behind the shop. Luke told her to take his wagon, and he would stay in the shack.

But Morning Star asked, "Can't I stay with you?"

Luke shuddered and said, "Aah . . . yeah!"

She led him into his lodge. She undressed and came to him; she spent the next several hours teaching him what she wanted him to do and how to make her feel like a woman. He became a man.

Later that night Luke held her in his arms as she slept and thought to himself, "Holy crap! I killed a man today and this has still been the best day ever."

But he had no idea how different his life would become in the near future.

Chapter 18

The next few days they rode their horses and laughed and packed things away in the wagon, spending all their time together, working and sleeping . . . they couldn't get enough of each other.

One afternoon Miguel came to Luke's wagon and handed him the sheath with the long rifle in it. He told Luke that this was a very special gun and that he had made some changes to it. Luke asked Miguel which one it was. Miguel smiled and said, "Oh, Señor Luke, eet is a little beet of each. You will not find another one like eet."

Luke looked at it and it truly was a beautiful weapon. He thanked Miguel for all the hard work. Miguel also handed Luke several boxes of cartridges and shotgun shells and told Luke to be sure and practice with the new rifle as it was unlike anything he has ever fired before.

Early the next morning, Luke hitched the mules to the new wagon. He was anxious to see what kind of problems he might encounter. He put Thunder on the left and Lightning on the right where they belonged, and they did not object. It was like they were waiting to go. Morning Star fixed some food for the day trip, and he tied her horse to the back of the wagon then climbed aboard, snapped the reins above the mule's rumps, and coaxed them on.

They headed north up the trail behind the buildings on the east side of town.

They had only traveled fifty feet or so when Storm came running up beside the wagon on Luke's side and moved in close so Luke could stroke his neck and talk to him. Then from nowhere Bear appeared at his heels and Luke said, "OK, you guys stay close," and they were off.

They rode for hours, crisscrossing the stream whenever he found a safe spot to see if there were any leaks. They ran the mules for a while to see how the new springs worked and what rattles popped up. Luke was very pleased at how well every part of the wagon responded. There were only a few minor adjustments for Gunther to make. Luke realized he would need more storage space if he were to do the things he had in mind. He thought about it and when they returned, he asked Gunther if there was a way to hook up the ox cart to the back of the wagon.

The next morning Gunther had added two 2x12 sideboards all the way around the cart with some hooks on the outside so Luke could carry cargo and keep it covered and out of the weather with a waterproof tarp.

Luke was getting ready for the adventure he had been dreaming of his entire life; he could feel the excitement rising.

The next couple of days were spent making final adjustments to the wagon, loading provisions, and talking with Teddy and Becky, making sure they had everything they needed for the shop. Teddy said he had come up with an idea that he'd tried over the last couple of weeks and it worked well. He had talked to some of the small ranchers about bringing their stock in for slaughter, and Teddy would do it for half the meat, no cost to the ranchers or farmers, and they would have meat to sell from the butcher shop at no cost to them. He would smoke the extra meat for them to come get as they needed it.

Luke liked the idea and gave Teddy and Becky his blessing, telling them if they had any other good ideas to go ahead with them. Mr. Weathers at the bank and Mr. Jones at the mercantile would give them whatever help they need.

"I've already talked with them," Luke said.

They said their goodbyes, and Luke told Teddy if he needed him to send telegraph messages to the towns between there and Denver, he would check for messages whenever he could.

Luke made a final check of the wagons and made sure the wheels were greased and the water barrel was full. He hitched up Thunder and Lightning, tied Morning Star's pony to the back of the ox cart, and told Teddy he expected to be gone a couple of months, more or less.

And they were off . . . .

Chapter 19

They moved north until almost sunset taking in every sound, sight, and smell; they couldn't have enjoyed their first day any more. Luke found a flat spot by the stream and a grassy meadow for the animals to graze. The higher they moved into the mountains the colder the nights and morning would be, even though it was the beginning of spring. He couldn't get over how well his new home had performed on the trail.

Luke made a fire in the stove, and the lodge warmed up quickly. At one point it got a little too warm, and he lowered the sideboards on one side. Morning Star cooked supper and they dined on smoked beef, squaw bread, and apricots that Mama B had canned before she died. Star made a pot of coffee, and they were in their lodge and life was good. Luke spent a few hours that evening by the oil lantern sketching his grandparents standing by their teepee with some horses in the background.

The pencil was something Luke had no access to and he had bought all that Mr. Jones at the mercantile had in stock. He had no idea how long one would last or how to use the eraser on the end, but he was getting familiar with them and Morning Star could not get over how real-looking his sketches were. They soon realized there was no reason to go to bed at sundown since they had light and a very warm and comfortable place to spend their time at night. Luke sketched till after midnight and they talked and laughed and finally turned in, both exhausted from the first day on the trail. Oh yeah!—and they made love.

The next morning before daylight, Luke stoked the fire, put a pot of coffee on, and tried to be very quiet so as not to wake Morning Star. Besides, he really enjoyed watching her while she slept; he couldn't believe how lucky he was to have such a beautiful woman at his side, one who loved the out of doors, loved animals, and loved to just wander at a slow pace, just the two of them. And, of course, Storm, Bear, Thunder, Lightning, and her paint pony.

She woke and fixed them a hot breakfast of maize with honey and ham. It was very cold outside the wagon, and they could hear Bear herding the mules and Storm around the meadow to warm them up and get them ready for a new day. Luke fixed a dish of cornmeal mush and ham for Bear, and he and the lady enjoyed another cup of coffee in no hurry to leave. When everyone was finished, Morning Star broke down camp. Luke hitched the mules, and they were off to nowhere in particular. What a great feeling, not having any place to be.

They had been on the trail for about two hours when shots rang out. They couldn't tell where they came from because of the echo through the forest. Three rounds hit the ground and kicked up dirt on the trail about fifteen feet ahead of the team. Luke looked in all directions as he pulled the wagon off the trail and up to the treeline by the stream. He took his Winchester, jumped on Storm, and told Morning Star to get a rifle, stay down, and keep alert.

Luke looked down at Bear and said, "Go find 'em, boy," and the large dog took off at a full run with Storm close behind. It wasn't long before Bear cut a fresh trail, turned to the northeast and headed toward the forest. Luke finally noticed what Bear was following and it looked like one person on a saddle horse and a pack horse, both animals without shoes, either an Indian or a mountain man.

They followed the trail deep into the forest and back up a canyon that Luke knew was at least five miles deep. They moved rapidly because the nights had been below freezing and every hoofprint jumped right out at him. There was a trail a little older coming down the canyon and one that was just a few minutes old going back up.

Bear growled, letting Luke know that they were getting very close. They went about fifty more yards, and Bear stopped and groused. Luke said, "I see him, fella," and he pointed for Bear to circle around to his right, get close, and hold. The big dog headed out at a full run into the heavy pine trees and out of sight. Luke swung his left leg over Storm's shoulders and slid down his right side to the frozen ground. Storm didn't mind him getting off the wrong side; Luke could do anything as long as it was with Storm.

By this time Luke was so mad he wasn't worried about being seen. He walked straight between the trees, dead straight at the camp. He saw a big man bending over, trying to start a fire. When he was about fifty yards out the big man hollered, "Come on in the camp, I been expectin ya!"

Luke was fuming and yelled, "Why the hell ya shootin' at us and whadya want?"

Luke pushed the safety off the shotgun in his holster.

The big man smiled an ugly grin that was just barely obvious under his heavy black beard, and then he said, "Ahh hell, squirt! I's just tryin' to get you up here out the way so's my two brothers could take a shot at yer woman. They took a likin' to her while's we was watchin y'all yesterday. Say! You ain't nothing but a young pup, you even shave yet?"

Truth was Luke hadn't shaved yet although he had begun to think about it as the fuzz on his chin was beginning to bother him. By this time Luke had moved within twenty feet of the camp, and the big man had made no aggressive moves, which had Luke kind of confused, although he didn't take his eyes off of the big man. When it finally dawned on him what he had said, he called to Bear who was standing about eight feet behind the trapper, and as he moved the big man jumped in surprise. He had no idea Bear was there.

Luke said to Bear, "Go help Star! Fast!" And the huge dog took off at full speed and disappeared into the pines in just a few strides. Luke said, "So you had me follow you up here, and what did you think was going to happen when I got here and found out what was happenin' to my woman?"

The big man just smiled that hairy, ugly grin once more and said, "Hell! I ain't afraid of you. In fact, I'll probably just kill ya and take yer gear and that great horse ya got. I'm purdy damn good with this six-shooter," as he put his right hand down close to the butt of his pistol.

Luke noticed the rawhide hammer strap that held his gun in place was off. He decided right there and then that if he was to do much gunfighting he was going to have to start paying more attention or this could be one of the shortest careers in the history of gunslingin'. That tickled him a little and he smiled, which took the big man by surprise. He asked, "What the hell you smilin' at, ya snot-nosed brat?"

Luke started to say that it was just an inside joke but before he could get it out the big man took that opportunity to pull his pistol.

Luke wasn't sure how it happened. He didn't feel his hand touch the grip of his sawed-off or his finger pull the front trigger, but he felt the twenty gauge jump against his right hip and saw the smoke and fire explode from the barrel. He saw the big man fly backward about six or eight feet and hit the ground with a thud, eight separate and individual holes in his belly and chest. As he fell backward, his reflexes allowed him to squeeze the trigger of his pistol, which was only a few inches above the top of his holster, and he shot himself in the right foot. Then his gun flew up in the air and over his head. He was lying on the ground and moaning, blood oozing out from under his back where four of the slugs had gone completely through and the other four were lodged in his chest.

Luke walked up to him, breaking open the shotgun, and replaced the spent twenty gauge shell. He closed the breech and pushed the safety back on with his right index finger. He looked down into the glazed eyes of the dying man who said, "Ahh hell, kid! What the hell didga shoot me with? I feel like I got six holes in me."

Luke replied without any emotion in his voice, "Nine if ya count yer foot."

The trapper laid there not able to move, dark, almost black blood from his liver and lung coming from his mouth. He said, "Don't leave me here like this. I can't stand this pain."

Luke said, "That's exactly what I'm gonna do, and if I thought it would make it hurt worse, I'd shoot ya a coupla more times," and he started to walk away. He took three steps and said out loud, "Ah hell!"

He turned on his heels and walked back to the trapper, pulled his knife as he approached the bearded man. He slit his throat and wiped his blade clean on the man's buckskin pants in one continuous stroke.

"I changed my mind," he said to himself.

Luke whistled, and Storm, who had been ground reined in the trees, jumped and headed for him. Luke jumped up on the big horse and settled himself.

As he patted his neck, he said to Storm, "Let's go find Star," and he gently nudged the horse in the flanks with the heels of his moccasins. Luke didn't try to guide him through the trees; he just gave him his head and let him pick his own trail. He knew they couldn't catch Bear as the dog was as fast as Storm and had several minutes' lead on them.

Storm seemed to sense the urgency of the situation, and he pushed on harder and harder without Luke coaxing him. They reached the site where Luke had left Morning Star and the wagon in record time. The first thing that Luke noticed was the mules still hitched to the wagon and trying to graze on the grass at their feet. Then he saw Bear straddling a man with his teeth bared ready to tear his throat out.

Luke rode up, skidded to a stop, and slid to the ground as he saw Morning Star in the tall grass off to his left. He told Bear to hold and the big dog growled as he put his mouth closer to the man's throat. The man was paralyzed and couldn't have moved if he had wanted to, which he truly didn't at this point.

Luke ran to Star and saw that she had been shot through the shoulder, both eyes were swollen shut, her nose was smashed and pushed to the right side of her face, she had several other bruises on her face, and her upper lip was split.

Her buckskin dress had been cut all of the way open and her breasts were exposed and covered in hand marks and bruises. She was unconscious and yet moaning.

As Luke tried to decide which of her wounds to treat first, he heard horses coming at a fast pace. He turned to see his uncle Wild Rider and two cousins riding hard in his direction. Luke put his thumbs against both sides of her nose and tried to straighten it back into place. He knew it wouldn't be perfect but hopefully it wouldn't be too noticeable. Luke told his cousin White Horse as he jumped down from his horse to get a towel from the wagon, take it to the stream, and get it wet. The icy water should help keep the swelling from getting much worse and slow the flow of blood.

His uncle saw the bullet wound and headed directly into the trees, returning in just a few minutes with several different kinds of moss and plants to make a poultice for her wounds. He laid the poultice on both sides of her shoulders where the bullet had entered and exited and then wrapped some of the towel into strips to hold the dressing in place.

Luke and his uncle took her to the wagon and laid her on the bed. Luke covered her with both heavy wool blankets and tucked her in tightly. He just stood and stared at her for several minutes, trying to keep the tears from welling up in his eyes. Finally, he stepped down from the wagon and asked his cousin White Horse to take her to the village and directly to his grandmother and tell her exactly what had happened; she would know what to do. Luke said, "Each time you stop to rest the mules, get fresh water for the towel on her face." White Horse assured him that he would.

White Horse headed the wagon north on the trail as fast as possible without causing Morning Star any more discomfort than necessary. She was still unconscious and moaning.

Luke walked over to where Bear stood straddling the trapper and said, "Bear, back!" and the big dog backed off the man just as Luke pulled his Colt .45 from the holster on his left hip and shot the man in his crotch.

The man screamed in agony and curled up into a fetal position. Luke then shot him in his left butt cheek.

The man screamed at Luke, "Don't! Please don't shoot me no more!"

Luke said, "Yeah, right!" and shot him in his left shoulder.

The man was rolling around on the ground in his own blood and screaming in pain.

Luke asked calmly, "Where did your brother go?"

The man replied, "I don't know!" and Luke shot him in the right shoulder.

The man howled in pain.

"I ain't gonna ask ya again," Luke said with his pistol cocked and ready to fire.

"OK! OK!" the man screamed, "he's headed for a shack we got about ten miles northeast of Taos just off the main trail."

Luke reloaded his pistol and put it back in his cross-draw holster. He bent down, took the skinning knife from his left moccasin, reached down, and grabbed the man's scrotum and penis, which had been exposed when Bear had hit him at full speed and knocked him about fifteen feet and then stood over him waiting for Luke.

Luke stood there holding the man's privates in his left hand and without any warning sliced through the flesh and cartilage as though it were soft butter. Blood squirted in all directions, and the trapper couldn't believe what was happening to him. As he continued to scream, Luke dropped the knife and grabbed the man's jaw with his right hand and held his mouth open while he stuffed the bloody appendage into his mouth with his left hand. The man started to reach for his mouth with the only working arm he had left, but Luke drew his pistol again and shot him in his right elbow. The man flopped back onto ground and passed out from the excruciating pain.

Luke asked his cousin Grey Wolf, who had been watching the whole event with great interest, to go and get the dead man and his rig from the canyon and bring him back here.

"What do you want me to do with this one here?" asked Grey Wolf

Luke replied, "He should be dead by the time you get back, but if by some chance he's not, cut his throat, tie him on his horse, and bring them both to that camp spot just outside of Taos. I'll meet ya there by sundown and if ya see Marshal Simms tell him yer waitin' for me and I'm on my way."

Grey Wolf agreed. He jumped on his pony and headed for the canyon to retrieve the first trapper's body and his rig.

Wild Rider asked Luke if he wanted him to cut the third trapper's trail and Luke said, "He won't be hard to find. He has Star's pony with him, so he won't be able to travel that fast, and besides I have Bear and he already has his trail. Just look at him . . . he's set to go."

Wild Rider looked south down the trail toward Taos and saw the very large dog up on his back legs, barking and begging Luke, "Come on, let's go!" Luke told his uncle that he was welcome to come along, but it was gonna be very simple.

"I'm gonna find him and kill him. I'm gonna shoot whatever part of him I see first, his back, his front, his head . . . I really don't care."

"I'll just ride along in case I can help " Luke's uncle said.

Luke grabbed the long rifle he had taken from the wagon, and laid it across his lap. They headed south trying to keep up with Bear.

They had been riding less than an hour when Luke saw Bear stop up ahead, turn, and look at him. He rode up close to the big dog, and Bear barked and looked down the trail. Luke looked close and could just make out Star's pinto pony and another horse and rider just ahead.

Wild Horse had just caught up with them when Luke said, "You better let yer horse get some air. We won't be too far ahead; this'll all be over in a couple of minutes."

Luke looked at Bear and said, "Let's go get him, boy," and Bear took off and was at a dead run in just three strides. Luke gave Storm his head and grabbed a hand full of mane. Storm fell in right behind Bear. They gained ground on the rider and the two horses to where Luke figured there was about four hundred yards between them.

"About another hundred-and-fifty yards," he thought. "I don't want to hit Star's pony by mistake."

Storm was really stretching it out, and Luke almost overrode the other trapper.

He saw the rider cut Star's pony loose, and it drifted off toward the stream for some water.

Luke pulled Storm up and slid off. He pulled his long rifle from the sheath and put together the two rods Gunther had made, driving the piece of equipment into the soft ground just off the trail. He chambered a fifty-two caliber shell and laid the barrel in the Y at the top of the rod, raising his sights for about two hundred yards, and took aim. He put the sight just about six inches outside the rider's right shoulder and squeezed the trigger slowly. The buffalo gun belched, exploded, and kicked the hell out of Luke's right shoulder. But Luke cleared the chamber, slid another round into the gun and took aim just in case the first slug missed. He focused and saw a riderless horse slow down and wander off the trail toward the stream.

Luke saw the man lying in the middle of the trail as the dust cleared. He was still moving but not much. Luke dropped his long gun on the trail and climbed up on Storm. They took off as fast as the great horse could run with Bear at his heels, barking his approval.

Just to be cautious, Luke began slowing Storm down about twenty yards from the man lying on the trail. He grabbed his Winchester by its sling and brought it over his shoulder to bear on his target as he chambered a round. He slid down off of his horse and walked up to the man. He saw that his hands were clinched together on his chest trying to stop the flow of blood that was gushing between his fingers. Luke sat down in the middle of the trail about three feet from the man and looked into his eyes.

"What the hell'd ya shoot me with, ya sons a bitch? Feels like all my innards are gone and I'm on fire."

"Yeah, a buffalo gun will do that to ya," said Luke.

"Ya gonna finish me off at least?" the dying man choked.

"Naw, you ain't worth the price of another bullet," Luke said as he looked the man in the eye with zero emotion. "Besides, you'll be dead in another ten minutes."

"Oh hell, mister, I'm in terrible pain, please!"

Luke looked at him and said, "Believe me, if I could think of a way to make you hurt more, you could bet yer dyin' ass I would, and you'd win the bet, too."

Luke watched him as blood filled the trail all around him and then started to soak into the dirt. He thought, "That's about all that separates the living from the dead is a gallon or so of blood.

Ain't much to show for a life," and then he lifted his Winchester and shot the mountain man in the forehead.

"I changed my mind again," he said to himself.

Wild Rider rode up with Luke's long rifle and the rest of his gear from the trail where he had shot the trapper. He had picked up Star's pony and was leading it as well. He looked down at the dead man and said, "Damn, boy, I sure hope I never make you mad, 'cause I know I can't outrun you and yer critters, and I sure don't want to get in a gunfight with ya."

Luke put his long rifle and rods back in the sheath and then started to get the trapper ready to be tied on his horse.

He didn't speak at all; he just looked south toward Taos for quite a while. Finally, when they had been riding for about thirty minutes, Luke said very nonchalantly, "Looks like were gonna beat Grey Wolf to the camp."

Chapter 20

It was close to three in the afternoon when Luke and Wild Rider reached the camp by the stream.

Luke left his uncle there to wait for Grey Wolf and the other two bodies while he rode into Taos to find Marshal Simms. He knew the marshal didn't like surprises and wanted to stay on his good side. Luke reined Storm up to the hitchin' post in front of the US marshal's office and slid down. He dropped the reins of the hackamore on the ground so Storm could reach the water trough under the hitchin' post. He walked up the steps and into Marshal Simms's office. Simms was already standing.

"Whatcha doin' back here so soon, young fella?" the marshal asked. Luke filled him in on the whole story.

The marshal asked if he had any idea who the three fellas were that Luke had sent to Purgatory, and Luke said, "In all the excitement I guess I forgot to ask."

Marshal Simms just smiled. He really liked this young man and he was startin' to think what it might be like if Luke wore a marshal's badge. It would sure take some of the pressure off of him, and he was beginning to realize that Luke was very capable of takin' care of himself.

Luke said, "I'll buy ya a drink if you'll ride out and take a look at these lost souls with me."

The marshal said, "Well let's go get that drink and talk it over."

They walked over to the saloon that had been painted and given a name, "The Welcome Inn," in bright red letters about a foot high painted over the swinging doors. Things had been cleaned up since the last time Luke had been there.

When they walked up to the bar, Harry the barkeep said, "Ya gonna be shootin' anybody in here today? Might get some curtains fer the winders if ya do," and he laughed a funny little laugh, "He He He!"

The marshal ordered some good whisky, and Luke ask Harry if the beer was cold and tossed him a five dollar gold piece. He grabbed the coin out of the air and said, "Yer damn right, ice cold! I keep it outside this time of year."

When the barkeep went out back to draw the beer from the crock and grab a bottle of his best whisky for the marshal, Luke said, "I really do need to get back on the trail to check on Star. I'm worried . . . she was beat up pretty good."

The marshal said, "You need to just relax a bit. From what I know of yer grandma, she's in the best possible hands."

Then Harry came back and set an extra-large schooner of beer in front of Luke and a clean shot glass and the bottle of whisky in front of the marshal.

Luke finished his beer, and the marshal finished four, maybe five shots of the best whisky he had ever drank. Luke told the barkeep to keep that bottle for the marshal, and the marshal smiled and said, "I'll be back directly."

They walked back to the office to get their horses and ride out to check on the three dead men.

They reached the camp and Grey Wolf had just arrived ten minutes earlier and was talking to his father.

The marshal took a look at the first dead man and went to the second. When he lifted his head, the marshal paused and turned to look at Luke; Luke just shrugged.

The marshal said, "Luke! Is that what I think it is in this feller's mouth?"

And Luke said, "I don't know, marshal. Just what exactly do you think it is?"

The marshal just grinned, checked the last man, and then said, "Goddamn, Luke, you just keep steppin' in horse crap and comin' out smellin' like lilac water. Do ya know who these fellers are?" Luke just shook his head; he had no idea.

"These here are the Winston boys. I been on the lookout fer them fer a couple of years. They all got paper on them, dead or alive, for shootin' up half of Albuquerque and killin' the sheriff and a US marshal while they was comittin' a bank robbery. I don't remember how much they're worth, but it's a hell of a lot more than you woulda made if you'd been workin' at the butcher shop today." They all smiled.

The marshal said, "I'll take these yahoos back to town and then send fer Gunther to come get their rigs and horses. Besides, I got a bottle of very good whisky with my name on it that I need to get back to."

Luke walked over and shook the marshal's hand. When the marshal took his hand away there was a fifty-dollar Double Eagle in his palm. He looked at Luke not knowin' what to say.

Luke said, "That should keep you in good whisky till I get back. And one more thing. Go through their pockets and whatever ya find I'll split it with ya."

The marshal smiled and said, "Ya got a deal," and he rode off toward town with the three dead men and their mounts in tow.

Luke said to his uncle and cousin, "We still have a couple of hours till dark. We need to head for the village."

They mounted their horses and headed north. They had been on the trail about thirty seconds when Luke realized that he last ate about daybreak and his stomach was starting to let him know. He also realized he'd left without his blanket or any provisions and that it was going to be a long, cold, hungry night . . . one more lesson learned and one mistake he wouldn't make in the future.

"Just take a minute to think what yer doin' and where yer goin'. Could save yer life," he thought to himself.

They stopped for the night at a spot that Wild Rider and Grey Wolf knew of, off the main trail about two hundred yards and out of sight.

"If someone was trying to hide for a while this would be a great spot," Luke thought to himself as he made a mental note of the place. "Could come in very handy."

They gathered wood and started a fire, larger than usual, and Luke was confused.

"Why so big?" he asked.

Wild Rider asked Luke to bring up about a dozen big rocks from the stream bed and put them in the fire pit, and it all started to make sense.

Grey Wolf had wandered off shortly after they arrived and was now coming back into camp with two very large rabbits. He headed for the stream to skin and clean them.

Luke thought, "I hate rabbit. How much worse can this get? Sleepin' on the cold ground *and* eatin' rabbit. Crap!"

Actually, the rabbit tasted pretty dang good.

"Musta been really hungry," he thought.

After they had eaten, Luke had fed Bear the leftover rabbit, which he devoured bones and all.

Luke's uncle started digging a trench with a tree branch, about six feet long, three feet wide, and about a foot deep. Luke followed suit and didn't have to ask why. He remembered his pa's teaching him this; his wildlife skills were all starting to come back to him.

When they had their trenches dug, they used their tree branches to drag the large rocks out of the fire and into holes they'd also dug. Then they covered them up with the dirt from the trenches. They walked down by the stream and picked an arm full of long grass and laid it onto the dirt on top of their trenches. They each piled firewood by the top of their beds so they could stoke the fire in the middle of the night without getting up.

They turned in, and Luke was surprised at how warm the bed was. The grass made it almost tolerable, too. They talked for a while but soon they were all sleeping heavily. Luke had only been asleep for a few minutes when he felt something against the small of his back. He reached behind him with his right hand and found Bear snuggling in. The big dog groaned once and they slept warm all night.

The next morning Luke and Bear were up at sunrise. Luke had decided to hit the trail before someone started to cook more rabbit. He asked his uncle and cousin if they would bring Star's pony along because he knew it would not be able to keep pace with Storm and Bear. They agreed, and Luke jumped up on Storm. Bear set the pace and in just a couple of minutes they were out of sight. They moved along very fast comfortably for the animals, and Luke just held on and let them run.

Luke rode into the Ute village in early afternoon. He saw his wagons on a flat area up behind his grandparents' lodge, and he noticed his mules down by the lake grazing in the meadow. The same young boy that had taken Storm the last time Luke came to the village was there to take the big horse again. Luke wanted to tell him to take special care of his horse, but he knew that was stupid; after all, "The People of the Horse."

Luke went to the front of his grandparents' lodge and called out, "Dark Moon! Are you there?"

As he was about to pull back the buffalo hide that covers the entrance, a voice from behind him said, "Of course I'm here. Where else would I be?"

Luke turned half startled. "How the hell do you do that?" he asked.

"Do what?" his grandmother asked with a faint smile.

"How is Morning Star?" he asked.

"She's resting, and it's going to take a couple of months for her to heal. She was in very bad condition when she arrived. I have given her something that will allow her to sleep. Right now rest is the most important thing for her."

"Where is she? Can I see her?" Luke asked.

"She is in your lodge and you be quiet! Do you hear me?" She glared at Luke and he replied, "Yes ma'am."

"I mean it!"

"Yes ma'am."

"I'll turn you into a toad if you wake her!"

"Yes ma'am."

And he walked away toward his wagons smiling; it was good to be back.

Luke quietly stepped into the wagon and watched her sleep.

Dark Moon had dressed the wounds and applied some sort of terrible smelling goo that seemed to be working. The swelling on her face had gone down quite a bit, her nose looked almost normal, and she was breathing very easily.

Luke watched her for about fifteen minutes and then left the wagon feeling much better about their future. He stepped down from the wagon and walked around his lodge and the ox cart to check on any damage that might have occurred on the hard trip. Everything seemed to be in good condition, but he would need to take it for a ride to be sure. That wouldn't happen, though, until Star was up and about.

As he checked his supplies and provisions on the ox cart it occurred to him that the young boy that was caring for Storm wasn't wearing a knife. He looked through his things in the ox cart and found the wooden box that had axes and knives. He found a skinning knife identical to the one in his legging, of the highest quality, and he found a sheath in another box that fit it perfectly. He also found a braided rawhide strap to use as a belt and he rolled it all together. He grabbed a handful of hard candy from the container he had purchased at Buck Jones's mercantile back in Taos. Putting them all in a leather pouch, he repacked the cart to protect everything from the weather then he headed down to check on his horse and dog.

He reached Storm who was grazing and enjoying the sweet grass. The animal looked like he had been given a bath; his coat was shining and his mane and tail had been brushed. He seemed ready for another trip. The big horse came to his side, and Luke scratched his neck, rubbed his muzzle, and fed him a piece of hard candy. Storm snickered. From out of nowhere Bear appeared to get his candy, and they sat down in the grass and relaxed for the first time in over twenty-four hours.

Luke saw the young boy walking toward them and when he got within ten feet Luke said to him, "Great job. He looks like he's been resting for days."

The young boy smiled and swelled with pride that the great Walks with Bears would even talk to him, let alone praise him for his work.

Luke handed him the leather pouch. The boy took it and looked at Luke with inquisitive eyes. Luke was pretty sure he had never received a gift before.

"Go ahead, open it," he said to the boy, who began to pull the ties on the pouch and reach inside. Luke saw his eyes get as large as wagon wheels when he pulled the knife and belt from the pouch.

He stuck a piece of hard candy in his mouth and said, "Walks with Bears, there must be some mistake. This can't be for me, it is too great a gift."

Luke said, "What is your name, little one?

The boy replied, "My name is Yellow Eagle."

Luke looked at him and said, "This is for you, there's no mistake. You're old enough to have your own weapon."

The boy beamed at the amazing present.

"How would you like to be the one in charge of caring for Storm and Bear?" Luke asked. "They are very special animals and need special care." Luke knew the boy would do a good job. He was raised to care for animals; it was in his blood.

"I would be very proud to take care of your animals," Yellow Eagle said as he sat down beside Bear and started stroking his head. "I may also need a friend if you have time. I haven't had time to make many friends lately," and the boy couldn't stop grinning.

As Luke walked back toward the village, he noticed the boy in the ice cold water giving Bear a bath, his first since he joined Luke and Storm.

That night Luke slept on a buffalo robe on the floor of the wagon beside Morning Star. Bear came into the wagon and slept at his feet. He was clean and smelled really good for a change. Yellow Eagle had rubbed him down with some kind of plant that made him smell almost floral, and Luke could tell he really enjoyed it. It was a very restless sleep, and Luke woke at sunrise feeling almost as bad as when he went to bed. He and Bear left the wagon very quietly and stretched as they walked, trying to get the knots out of their muscles.

Luke realized that he had gone the whole day before without eating and headed straight for the cook fires. As he approached, Yellow Eagle appeared by his side with a giant wooden bowl of maize and meat for Bear, and Luke said, "WOW! Maybe I should have you take care of me, too."

The boy smiled and replied, "I can do that if you want!"

Luke said, "We'll see," and walked on to the cook fires to get a bowl. He ate like a starved man. He had two bowls of maize and some roasted antelope, and a large bowl of wild berries with goat's milk on them. He was just finishing his meal when his uncle came up and joined him.

"How are you, Walks with Bears?" he asked, concerned.

Luke said, "I'm fine now that I know that Star is going to be OK. What time did you get to the village?"

"Before sundown," Wild Rider said. "We didn't want to bother you. We knew you had a great deal on your mind."

"Thank you for all your help," Luke replied. "I owe you a great debt, and I will never forget what you and your sons have done for me."

They talked for a while then shook hands the Indian way and parted.

As Luke walked back to his grandparents' lodge he noticed his wagon move just a little and he headed in that direction. Before he got close Morning Star came around the corner bracing herself against the side with one hand. Luke rushed to her side and grabbed her just before she collapsed in his arms. He sat on the tung of the wagon and held her in his arms.

She looked into his eyes and said, "Good morning," and smiled. He kissed her forehead, her nose, gently, and her lips; she moaned softly.

He said, "I was so worried."

"What about my pony?" she asked.

Luke told her the whole story, not leaving out a single detail. She wept, not so much in sadness but more from joy because those bastards had been put down.

She ate and then rested, and as the days passed she got stronger almost every day.

Luke could almost see her improve by the hour; he was never out of shouting distance.

Early one morning Luke awoke, and she was gone from the wagon. He dressed, went outside, and found her sitting on her pony with Storm standing beside them.

"How about a ride she said?"

"Nothing I would rather do," replied Luke.

He jumped from the wagon onto Storm's back and settled in. They rode toward the forest.

"How are you doin'?" Luke asked as they rode for the trees.

"I'm fine but I'm starving," she said.

"You should have thought of that before we left the village."

"I did," she said and showed Luke the large pouch that was slung over her shoulder.

They stopped at their favorite spot by the stream. They ate squaw bread and smoked turkey. Luke walked into the woods and picked some wild berries. He thought out loud, "Here I am sitting on the damned ground again. Why didn't we take the wagon?"

Morning Star looked him in the eyes and said in a very soft voice, "Shut up and make love to me."

And he did.

Chapter 21

Later that afternoon when they returned from their ride, Luke moved the wagons up the trail and maneuvered them into their spot by the stream. If Luke could only pick one spot to spend the rest of his life this would be it. Morning Star couldn't have been more pleased. Bear, Storm, the mules, and her pony all seemed to like the idea as well: lots of grass and water and life was good.

Luke was in the mood for some fresh trout, and in fifteen minutes he had three very large rainbows lying on the bank. He built a fire in the pit outside and retrieved the grate that Gunther had made to lay across the pit. He cleaned and fileted the fish and laid them on the grate skin down while Star made squaw bread and a pot of coffee on the small stove.

She laid out tin plates and forks on the bed. When the fish were grilled, she handed a plate out the folding window and Luke put two on the plate and the third one he put on the grass for Bear. Star threw a large piece of squaw bread out the window to go with Bear's fish. Luke handed Star the fish and climbed up into the wagon. Star pulled the window up by the rawhide cord and latched it on the inside. Luke could tell the night was going to be very cold, so he made plans to get a supply of firewood inside the wagon before they retired for the evening.

He also put up the canvas that fit the side of the wagon. It hooked to some metal poles that Gunther had forged to make a lean-to down either side of the wagon depending on where the wind and cold were coming from. This allowed him to get the stock out of the weather.

Morning Star turned in early and fell off to sleep instantly while Luke did some sketching by the oil lamp. He slept on the floor again not wanting to disturb her rest. He thought she might be rushing her recovery.

During the night a spring storm hit their camp and changed everything into a winter wonderland. Sometime in the middle of the night Bear pushed the trap door in the floor open and snuggled on the buffalo robe with Luke. He woke up long enough to throw some more wood into the stove, and their lodge stayed nice and warm for the rest of the night.

Luke woke just after daylight and looked out to find everything covered in snow. So he threw some more wood on the fire, filled the coffee pot with snow and water from the barrel, and made a pot of coffee. He was sitting against one of the cabinets wrapped in the buffalo robe and sipping a cup of coffee when Star woke and said, "That smells wonderful. Can I have some?"

Luke handed her the cup and she took a sip and sighed in ecstasy.

"Oh that's every bit as good as it smells."

"How are you feeling?" he asked.

She smiled and said, "After the night's sleep I just had, how could you feel anything but incredible? What are our plans for today?" she asked.

Luke reached across her and dropped the panel of the wagon down enough for her to see and feel the chill.

"Oh," she said, "maybe you should come back to bed. Looks like we're gonna be holed up for a while."

That was the best idea Luke had heard in a long while. He dragged the buffalo robe onto the bed with him. They drank coffee and rested in each other's arms for most of the morning.

Luke finally had to go and check the horses and team and relieve himself. He cleared most of the snow off the cover for the ox cart and brought the makins' for some squaw bread and a large cast iron frying pan along with some smoked ham. When he climbed back in the wagon Star had fallen off to sleep again but she had a big smile on her face. Luke put everything aside for the time being, stoked the fire, and poured himself another cup of hot coffee. He looked through his sketchbook to see if any of his pictures needed some finishing touches, but each one felt finished to him.

Most of them were of Star. He just stared at them and thought how lucky he was to still have her.

That afternoon the sun came out, and by four o'clock all the snow was melted. He moved the stock back across the trail so they could graze.

Star poked her head out of the wagon and hollered at Luke, "Hey! Ain't you ever gonna feed me?"

"Well, I was thinkin' about it but I couldn't wake yer lazy ass up."

"Well it's up now, so let's eat," she replied.

Luke had walked up the mountain and found where some quail were nesting. He relieved them of half-dozen eggs. He fixed squaw bread, ham, and scrambled eggs, made another pot of coffee, and they ate.

It was almost sunset when Yellow Eagle wandered into their camp.

"Hello," he yelled, "anybody at home?"

Luke stuck his head out the back door of the wagon. "Hey little one. Where ya been?" he asked.

"Well! If you would tell the help where yer off to it would be a whole lot easier for them do their job!"

Luke grinned and said, "Yer right. I'm sorry, I got so busy I completely forgot."

"It's OK," answered Yellow Eagle. "I brought some grain but not enough for the mules and Star's horse."

Luke noticed that he was on foot and asked, "Where's yer horse?"

"I don't have one. My father is very sick and has been crippled for several years. He has not been able to hunt or fish, and our only food is what the other families leave for us. My father is a very proud man and doesn't like to accept charity. My mother cries at night when she thinks no one can hear."

Luke asked, "Don't you have a rifle?"

Yellow Eagle said, "No, we are very poor and don't have anything to trade to get things like that."

Luke thought for a moment and then said, "Take Star's horse and go back to the village. Be ready to ride at sun up."

The young boy fed the grain to Storm and then jumped on the pinto pony and rode back to the village.

Luke walked back to the wagon and Star was waiting for him.

"Did you give my pony away?" she asked indignantly.

Luke said, "Aaah . . . no, not exactly. He's just borrowing it until I can get him a horse of his own. We're leaving early in the morning to find the wild herd and get him a mount. You'll have the whole day to be able to rest and enjoy this incredibly beautiful spot."

"Yeah! Yeah!" she exclaimed sarcastically with a grin on her pretty face.

Luke decided to try and change the subject. He retrieved his drawing pad from under the bed and showed her pictures he had done in the last week while she slept.

"Isn't that the hill behind the butcher shop?" she asked.

"Yes, and what do you think about the cabin?"

"It's very beautiful," she replied. "The corral and barn and stable look very well made."

Then he turned the page and showed her the design for the inside of the cabin. She looked with amazement at the very large bedroom upstairs, the large room downstairs with a two-story fireplace, and a kitchen with a sink, large cook stove, and a dining area. She was confused.

"What is this all about?" she asked.

"Do you think you could live in this place in the winter?" Luke asked.

"What do you mean?"

"If you could be happy living there in the winters, then I will have it built."

"How can you get all these wonderful things?" she asked.

Luke said, "Ah . . . I guess we need to talk."

He explained how Papa Jo and Mama B had left all their possessions and wealth to him, making him a very rich man, and now she is a very rich lady. He had plenty of money coming in from the town even though he wasn't there. After they finished dinner Luke went out to check on the stock and get the ropes and supplies ready for the ride in the morning. He went to the ox cart and found an almost new Winchester and a sling for it. He set a couple of boxes of shells and the rifle just inside the wagon door, ready for the ride in the morning.

Morning Star said, "You're a very kind and generous person, Luke Kash," and he blushed a little.

"Well, they need my help! And what good does it do to have things if you can't enjoy them with your friends?" he observed.

"I like that, very much," she replied.

The next morning before daylight, Luke rode out on Storm with Bear running by their side. He had two lariats and a couple of lead ropes as well as his Winchester and a large pouch over his left shoulder. Inside the pouch were some smoked meat and some squaw bread that Star had packed.

He had extra shells for his rifle and the two boxes of shells for the rifle he had brought for Yellow Eagle.

He arrived at the village just as the sun was coming up, and Yellow Eagle was standing by Star's pony raring to go.

"Did you eat?" asked Luke and Yellow Eagle assured him that he had. Luke handed him the extra rifle and rode off to the northeast. When the boy caught up he had a strange look on his face.

"Walks with Bears! What is this for?" he asked.

"It's for killing food," Luke replied.

"I know that, but why did you have me carry it?"

"Because you don't have one," Luke said and kept riding.

He nudged Storm with his heels, and the big horse changed gaits to a fast gallop. Yellow Eagle had to coax Star's pony to keep up.

They rode for almost two hours before they reached the waterhole where the wild herd stayed. They stopped up on the hill about five hundred yards from the grazing herd, and Luke asked Yellow Eagle if he saw a particular horse that he liked. The boy looked at all the horses and finally pointed out a buckskin that caught his eye.

Luke looked at it for a couple of minutes and then said, "Look at its left front leg. He favors his left side when he walks, and it looks like a permanent injury. That horse will not serve you very well." Yellow Eagle looked and saw the problem with the horse.

"Which one would you pick for yourself?" he asked.

Luke looked carefully and then said, "See the young palomino standing on the other side of the pond with its rump to us? See the conformation of its chest and shoulders and how well formed his rump is?"

"Yes, yes I do," said Yellow Eagle.

"That horse will run all day and all night without tiring. He may not be the fastest horse in the herd, but he will serve you very well for many years."

The boy agreed.

"Can you use a lasso?" asked Luke and the boy answered affirmatively.

Luke showed him where he was to hide in the reeds on this side of the pond, explained how they would herd the horses, and how he was to head back to the reeds when he and Bear had the horse separated from the herd.

"You must be very quiet until the very second you are ready to throw yer rope, and as soon as yer rope is over his head start talking to him and don't stop. Keep walking up the rope and talking to calm him down. You'll be on yer own.

"Bear and I won't be able to help you, so stay alert to what is going on around you."

Yellow Eagle nodded that he understood. Luke and Bear headed down the hill to circle around to the far right while the boy headed down the hill toward the water hole.

When Luke was in position, he signaled and all three of them started off at a full run to turn the herd and work their way to separate the palomino. The roundup went just as Luke had described it to the boy, and when Luke and Bear got back to the waterhole Yellow Eagle was standing out in the grassy area holding his left hand out to the young horse and holding the lasso in his right. The horse was a little nervous and fidgety, but the boy was doing a great job of quieting him.

Luke pulled Storm and Bear up to a stop about fifty yards from them, slid off of his horse, and stood very still until he was sure Yellow Eagle had the young horse under control. Then he started walking very slowly toward them, keeping Bear and Storm by his side so as not to spook the new horse. He called to Yellow Eagle, "When you think he is calm enough, walk him over to the trees and tie him off."

Luke showed him how to walk around the horse with his hand on his withers and rump, the points of his shoulders, and his flanks, all the while talking to him in a very calm voice.

Luke finally said, "Let him rest and calm down. You can come help me get that beautiful grey down there."

They repeated the exercise, except this time Luke came back to hide in the reeds while Yellow Eagle and Bear brought the part of the herd with the grey in it back to the waterhole.

When Luke had finished calming the grey and had it tied to the tree with the palomino, he took the boy up the hill for some target practice with his new rifle. Most Indians were terrible shots with guns of any kind. They never seemed to get used to the sound of the explosion when it fired. Most of them were at least very apprehensive. Not so with Yellow Eagle. He seemed to relish the recoil and would pull the rifle back into his shoulder, ready for the next shot. He was a natural.

They rode back toward the village with the two new horses in tow, talking and laughing and arguing like old friends, which is what they felt like.

Before he left for his camp, Luke gave the young boy some helpful hints on ways to hurry up the horse's training and then said, "Don't forget to come up and feed the stock and give Storm a rubdown."

"I'll be there just as soon as I get Gold Eagle hobbled down by the lake," said Yellow Eagle.

"I'll see you soon, and be sure to tell your mother and father you'll be bringing some fresh meat home for dinner tonight."

Yellow Eagle smiled with pride.

Three days later, after Morning Star had spent time visiting with her parents and Luke had spent time with his grandparents and cousins, he went through the wagons to make sure everything was trail ready, all the wheels greased and everything tied down and secure. They headed for Taos, but this time there was Storm, Bear, Thunder and Lightning the mules, Star's pony, and the big grey. After being around the grey for several days, Star was becoming very fond of the new horse, and vice versa.

Luke had a feeling she would; he had picked the horse especially for her. They camped that night in the spot a couple of hundred yards off the trail that Wild Rider had shown Luke the last time they rode to the village from Taos.

Morning Star loved the camp as much as Luke, Bear, and the stock did.

Luke caught trout, and they had hot squaw bread, carrots, potatoes, and hot coffee. Everyone slept very sound and warm in the lodge that night, Bear on his bearskin rug on the floor.

They got back on the trail a couple of hours after sunup and traveled slow but steady all day. It was about three in the afternoon when Luke noticed dust coming from the trail up ahead. He couldn't see anyone yet, but he had the feeling there was more than one rider. He asked Star to grab the shotgun and be prepared. A few minutes later Luke could see that there were three riders coming at a fast gallop. Luke pulled the wagons to the far right just off the trail to allow them to go by.

The trail riders slowed their horses as they approached Luke's wagons, and all three took a hard look at Star and Luke as they rode by.

Luke could tell they were checking out the wagon and the ox cart, and he felt uneasy about the riders. When they were out of sight, he told Star to double check the shotgun and get ready.

"For what?" she asked.

"They'll be back very soon," he said.

"How do you know?"

"A gut feeling, he said. "Just stay alert."

Ten minutes later, Bear began to bark, and Luke said, "I know, I know. Just be ready." And the big dog barked his understanding.

"Point that scattergun at the chest of the one closest to you, and if anyone starts to make a move, pull the front trigger and then the second. Don't wait for them to start shootin'. Do you understand?"

Star shook her head and seemed very calm; her eyes started to turn black.

Luke had never seen this side of her before. He was glad that there was no fear there, but he still didn't know what to expect from her.

The three riders came up fast. Two went by on Luke's side of the wagon, and the third went by on Star's side. They rode fast, went about thirty yards past, and pulled up hard and turned around to face Luke's wagon. Then they started walking back their way.

Luke stepped down from the wagon, pushed the safety of his scattergun with his right index finger, and stood in the middle of the trail.

Star stayed seated with the twelve-gauge, double-barrel scatter gun at the ready, both hammers cocked back. Two of the riders stopped about ten feet from Luke, and one stopped on Star's side of the wagon about the same distance. He was the first to speak.

"How you folks doin' this fine day?" he asked with a smug look on his face.

Luke turned to look at him without letting the other two men out of his peripheral vision.

"We're doin' just fine. What can I do for ya?" he asked.

The single rider seemed to be the boss man; the other two waited for him to speak.

"Why, hell! Yer just a baby, I guess we'll just take whatever you got, then I think I'll show yer lady what a growed-up man is like."

Luke didn't hear so much as feel Star raise the scattergun a few inches and pull the trigger, hitting the lone rider full in the chest and knocking him backward off of his horse. He landed on his neck on the dusty trail.

Luke heard the crack as he hit the ground and laid deathly still. At the same time all this commotion was going on, the man closest to Luke was trying to draw his pistol. Luke moved his hand down to the grip of his gun, pushed the handle down until it was in position, and squeezed the front trigger. The man facing him caught seven of the eight slugs from Luke's blast in his stomach and chest and was knocked sideways off his horse. The last slug just caressed his horse's neck and sent him into a bucking and fishtailing frenzy. The bucking horse kicked the third man's horse that was directly behind him, and that started the last horse to bucking as the man was just getting ready to pull the trigger on

Luke. But the bullet went wide right, hitting Luke in the left arm just below the shoulder. It went through but didn't hit any bone.

The man was holding on with all his might while he was firing wildly in all directions, trying to stay on top of his mount. He finally got his horse under control as he fired the last shot in his pistol. He turned his horse and spurred it hard toward Taos.

Luke called to Bear who was under the wagon, "Go get him, boy," and the great dog leapt into action. The lone rider had covered less than fifty yards when Bear overtook him and jumped onto the back of his horse at a full run. He had his mouth around the man's neck as he pulled him off his horse and landed on top of him when he hit the ground, never to see another sunrise.

Bear started walking back to the wagon, the bad man's horse in tow, to check on his family.

Luke asked Star what happened that caused her to pull the trigger.

"He said he was going to rape me, and that is never ever going to happen again," she said.

"Well, that's three that will never get to admire your beauty anymore," Luke said as he smiled at her.

They gathered the two horses and tied them to the wagon, and then they tied the men down tight to their mounts. Bear came trotting up with the third horse, the reins hanging loosely in his mouth.

Star made Luke sit still long enough for her to dress the wound in his arm. Luke resisted so she poked the hole in his arm with her finger. He jumped and said, "OK! OK!"

They all headed down the trail toward Taos to check on the man that Bear had dealt with.

Luke approached cautiously although he was sure the man was already sitting beside Lucifer's chair.

Luke had sifted through the men's pockets and come up with a very nice gold watch and chain—probably stolen—three-hundred twenty dollars in cash, three pistols and holsters, a couple of knifes, and three Winchesters.

They weren't really outfitted for hunting or trapping but looked like plain old robbers and maybe killers. More than likely they all had some paper on them, and Luke and Gunther would add some guns and some good saddle horses and tack to their sales business.

They rode into Taos about four hours later looking like a gypsy caravan—a wagon, an ox cart, three horses with no riders, and three horses with bodies tied to them.

US Marshal Brady Simms was standing in front of his office with a big ol' smile on his face as they approached.

"Who ya got there, young lad?" Marshal Simms asked.

"Don't have a clue," replied Luke, "they just came at us back up the trail, and the one on the bay started to tell Star what he was gonna do to her after they killed me, and that was his first and last mistake."

Simms walked out, raised each dead man's head, and said, "Luke, I swear I don't know how you do it. These three are part of a gang that robbed the bank in Santa Fe a coupla days back. Killed the banker, a barkeep, wounded the sheriff, and raped a couple of the whores. I just got the paper on them this morning. They're all wanted dead or alive, five hundred dollars each."

Luke smiled and said, "Looks like we're gonna be drinkin' good whisky for a while longer."

The marshal smiled and said, "I'll make out the paperwork for you to sign and get yer money to ya in the mornin'."

"Just give it to Mr. Weathers at the bank. Have the undertaker pick up these hombres." Luke tossed him a fifty-dollar gold piece. "That should cover it. I'll send Gunther up for their rigs in a little bit. Let me get Star settled in and say howdy to Teddy and Becky, then I'll meet ya over at Harvey's place for a drink in an hour or so."

The marshal agreed, and Luke and his troop headed on down the main street to the livery.

Gunther and Miguel saw them coming, and they were waiting as they pulled up to the front doors of the livery.

"Looks like ya got some new stock since the last time I saw ya," Gunther said.

"Yeah, we're gonna sell Star's paint and keep the big grey for her. There's a bunch of guns and stuff in the back for you to take a look at," Luke said to Miguel, and he smiled.

"Jes sir, mister Luke."

About that time Teddy and Becky came walking up from the butcher shop. They helped Star down from the wagon and walked her back to the shop for some rest.

Luke finished telling Gunther and Teddy about the three men and their gear and ask Gunther if he could have the carpenters meet him in the morning to talk about the new cabin. Then he went to the shop to have something to eat and some hot coffee. Luke asked Teddy about the shop and business. He was pleased to find that everything was going very well and that they were truly happy to be there. Luke was very happy to have them.

They fixed Star a hot bath and told Luke that Becky would fix something special for dinner.

While Star soaked, Luke walked down to the Welcome Inn to meet Marshal Simms and have a couple of snorts to get some of the trail dust out of his throat. Luke told Simms and Harvey about his plans to build up on the hill overlooking the town and that he was anxious to get started. Luke drank his cold beer and several locals came up to shake his hand and tell him how happy they were to have him back. He felt very good about calling Taos one of his homes.

When he returned from his meeting with the marshal, he found Star wearing one of her new dresses. She was truly lovely. Dinner was incredible, and life was very good.

Chapter 22

Three weeks later the log cabin was nearing completion. There was a covered porch that ran all the way across the front and down the right side so Luke and Star could sit out front and look down on the town or sit on the side and watch the corral and stables. Luke had one of the carpenters make a half-dozen rocking chairs, and Miguel made stuffed leather cushions for each one. The head carpenter built a very large bed of crosscut planks, and Luke ordered a custom-made mattress to fit.

Gunther made a very special cook stove like nothing Luke had ever seen and also supervised the building of the fireplace. A week later they moved into their new home. It was finished two weeks ahead of time because Luke and Star got so excited that he hired six more men to help with the project, then he kept them on to finish the barn, stable, and corral. When the work was complete, Luke made sure every worker was paid a very nice bonus. He kept two of the men that he had become good friends with as full-time workers at the ranch. They were handy with a pistol and rifle and were loyal to Luke and Star.

He had a bunkhouse built out of logs as well, with four individual rooms and a common area. He built it back under some pine trees, and it was a perfect addition to the ranch. It hadn't started out as a ranch; it just kept morphing as the work progressed and Luke kept making changes.

One late afternoon Luke had invited Teddy, Becky, and Marshal Simms for dinner. After eating a wonderful meal of grilled venison, wild asparagus, wild greens, and nuts with fresh fruit that Morning Star had prepared to perfection, the men were sitting on the porch in rocking chairs, enjoying some very good brandy and cigars that Luke had ordered from the East to have on hand for evenings like this.

They were watching the sunset over Taos and enjoying the view when Brady Simms spoke up.

"Luke, ya know, Taos is growing by leaps and bounds, and my job is startin' to get ahead of me. What I'm tryin to say is, I could use a hand, and I think yer the man fer the job."

This caught Luke completely off guard, and he was at a loss for words for a few seconds.

"Wow! I didn't see that comin'. Where did you come up with this idea?" he asked.

"Well," Brady said, "Yer well respected around these parts, and you definitely can handle yerself. I know I can trust you to do whatever ya say. So in my mind that makes you the man fer the job."

Luke thought out loud, "Luke Kash, US marshal. It does have a nice ring to it," then said, "But I'll need to talk it over with Star, and I may have some conditions. Whadya think, Bear?"

The big dog barked his approval and lay back down at Luke's feet.

Brady shook his head and said he understood.

"Why don't you come by my office tomorrow after you sleep on it, and we'll hash out the details." Luke agreed.

They spent the next couple hours enjoying each other's company and making small talk while Star and Becky strolled around the ranch.

The next morning just after sunup, Luke brought out Storm and the big grey horse. He and Morning Star rode up into the wilderness behind the ranch and into parts of their property that Star hadn't seen or realized they owned. They picked apples and apricots and some prickly pears. She still had trouble believing that one man could own so much and be so wealthy. They talked and laughed for several hours before returning to the ranch.

Luke returned the big grey to the corral where he rubbed him down and gave him a bucket of grain. They had a meal on the porch and then Luke, Storm, and Bear headed down the hill to meet with Marshal Brady Simms.

"Come on in and get yerself a cup of coffee," said the marshal.

Luke handed him a bottle of good whisky and said, "How about a shot of this in yers to sweeten it up a bit?"

The marshal smiled and said, "I like yer style," then he asked Luke what he and Star had decided.

"Well," Luke replied, "I ain't really lookin' fer a job, but I do owe ya some favors. So I guess if you can agree to a couple of conditions we might be able to do this."

"What do ya need from me?" the marshal asked.

"Well, I kinda got used to the money and the hardware I've been collectin' from the outlaws around here, and I know marshals ain't allowed to collect bounties."

The marshal scratched his head, thought a minute, then said, "How about if you should find yerself in the position where you have to take down a bad man or two, you have Morning Star bring 'em in for the bounty?"

"That's not a bad idea."

"What else," Brady asked.

"Well, if you need me to travel, I take my wagon. I'm spoiled ya know. I like my comfort."

"I certainly don't see a problem there. In fact, that'll save me money on room and board."

"So what kind of money does a federal lawman make?" Luke asked.

The marshal replied, "It's usually two hundred a month plus expenses, but since you already have a home and place to chow down, I guess we're gonna have to give you a little extra. How about two seventy-five a month and your expenses when yer on the trail?"

Luke thought for a minute then said, "Well, I guess we got a deal."

Brady Simms stood and asked Luke to do the same and raise his left hand. He quoted the oath, and Luke agreed to uphold his new position. When they finished, Brady shook Luke's hand and said congratulations to Luke Kash, United States federal marshal.

Two days later Marshal Simms came by the ranch early in the morning, and Luke had hot coffee and griddle cakes waiting. As they ate, the marshal told Luke he was on his way to Albuquerque to handle some trouble. Luke asked if he needed him to go along and Brady said, "Naw! One problem, one marshal that's how it usually works. Besides, yer in charge here. If I need ya I'll send you a telegram."

The marshal jumped up in the saddle and turned his horse south. He waved goodbye to Luke, and a few minutes later he was out of sight.

Luke felt kind of uncomfortable walking around town with a bright, shiny, silver marshal's badge pinned to his shirt, but the town folk all seemed to be happy that Luke was around and on the job. They smiled and waved and said hello, and he began to adjust to his new position in the community.

A couple of days passed and Luke started to get that feeling he got when trouble was on the horizon. He and Bear walked around town but couldn't detect anything out of the ordinary. He stopped by the telegraph office just as the messenger came running out and ran right into Luke.

"Oh, marshal!" the young lad said. "I was just on my way to find you. You have a message from Marshal Simms."

Luke took the slip of yellow paper, unfolded it, and studied the words.

"Two bad men headed yer way, stop. Killed 3, stop. Watch yer back, stop. Robbed & killed rancher and raped wife and daughter, stop. On my way, stop."

"When did this come in?" Luke asked the operator.

"Just a few minutes ago," he replied.

"Thanks," Luke said.

He left the office and headed down the street to the marshal's office.

Luke had been sitting at the desk in the marshal's office for about two hours, going through wanted posters and memorizing faces and names when he heard hoof beats. He looked out the window and saw two riders on lathered-up horses going past the office and reining up to the Welcome Inn saloon.

Luke watched them slide down from their horses and throw their reins over the hitchin' post. The two horses went right for the water trough.

Luke could tell the horses had been ridden way too hard for their own good and probably hadn't been feed properly, either. This in itself was enough to make Luke's blood boil.

"Ya need to take care of yer stock if you want them to take care of you," he angrily said to himself and thought of his pa.

The two men were laughing and patting each other on the back as they walked into the saloon knowing there was no law in town since they left the marshal in Albuquerque last night and rode like blazes. They walked up to the bar, and Harry Vaughn took one look and knew they were trouble.

"What can I get you fellers?" he asked.

"You got cold beer and good whisky?" one of the riders asked.

"You got cash?" asked Harry, expecting a Colt .45 across his cheek.

"We'll take two beers and a bottle of yer best, and make it quick. We're plum parched."

The rider doing all the talking took a ten-dollar gold piece from his pocket and threw it on the bar. Harry came back with the two beers, two clean shot glasses, and a bottle of his best whisky and set them on the bar.

"What do we owe ya?" the talkative rider asked.

"Fifteen cents for the beer and four dollars for the bottle . . . four dollars and thirty cents," Harry said still not sure what was coming next. He reached for the coin and the quiet man pulled a skinning knife and drove it through Harry's hand. Harry screamed in pain.

"Just leave it there. We'll let you know when we're through," he said. The man pulled the knife out of Harry's hand and wiped the blood on Harry's sleeve.

Harry grabbed a bar towel and wrapped it around his hand to try and stop the bleeding.

Luke walked out of the office and across the street, pausing by the two horses that were still drinking water. He patted their necks and looked closely at their hooves, they were worn and in need of new shoes.

"Disgusting," he thought to himself as he walked up the steps.

With his index finger he pushed the safety off of the over-and-under in his holster and walked through the swinging doors into the saloon. Luke kept his eyes on the two trail hands and saw the blood on the towel wrapped around the Harry's hand.

He moved to his left as he walked through the doors and asked, "You OK, Harry?"

"Hell no, I ain't OK! This somebitch stuck his pig sticker in my hand for no reason."

The two men didn't turn to check on Luke. They just worked on their drinks. Luke moved up to the bar about fifteen feet from the two saddle tramps.

"What's goin' on here?" Luke asked with authority in his voice.

"Who's askin'?" the man closest to Luke said.

"That'd be me, I guess!"

"And just who the hell are you?" asked the man at the bar.

"US Marshal Luke Kash."

Both men turned to look at Luke.

"What do ya want with us?" the first man asked.

Luke said, "I should arrest you two for the way you've treated yer mounts and for putting a knife in Harry's hand, but I'm afraid that's the least of yer problems."

"Run along, youngin', and you might live to play yer games another day."

"So you think robbin' and killin' a rancher and rapin' and killin' his wife and young daughter is some kind of a game?"

Luke asked "You both have paper on ya for cattle rustlin' and stealin' horses. One hundred fifty each. But I'm pretty sure the new posters will be over five hundred. They should be here by the time we bury yer sorry carcasses."

"What do ya mean 'bury,' ya young pup?"

"Well, the way I see it, yer either comin' with me to the jail to wait to be hanged, or yer gonna die right here where ya stand."

"You gonna draw on the both of us?" the first man asked without concern.

"That's up to you," Luke replied.

"What the hell is that contraption in yer holster? Ya think yer gonna clear leather with that long-ass thing?" Both men looked at each other and snickered. "We're pretty damn good with these sixguns, and you sure as hell ain't takin' us to jail, that's for sure."

"Well, that's really up to you," and Luke's eyes turned cold and dark.

The two men looked for some sign of fear in Luke's face, but all they saw was death, and they wondered what they had come up against. Luke stood as still as a statue with his hand poised just above the grip of his scattergun. The silence was deafening.

That's when Harry dropped the beer schooner he held in his hand. When it hit the floor all hell broke loose. Both men were going for their guns and trying to see what happened behind them. Harry dove for the floor as Luke's scattergun exploded, one barrel then the other. The two men had their pistols almost clear of their holsters when sixteen pieces of lead tore through their guts, knocking them backward off their feet and onto the floor. One of the sixguns went off and hit the first man in his right foot before he dropped it to the saloon floor. The other man still had a hold of his gun as he landed on the floor and the first man landed on top of him. Both men were screaming in excruciating pain.

Luke popped the breach on his twenty gauge and reloaded it as he walked over to the pile of humanity bleeding all over the saloon floor.

"Oh, you sonofabitch !" one of the men sputtered in a voice that was barely audible. "What the hell did you do? I ain't never seen nothing like that in my life."

"And you never will again," Luke said in a calm voice.

"Ain't you gonna get us a doc?" the man said.

And Luke replied, "No! I'm gonna sit right over there and drink a beer and watch you no good bastards bleed out. And I hope it takes a long time. Harry! You better go over to the doc's and have that hand looked at. I'll stay here and keep an eye on things."

Harry started to walk out the swinging doors and Luke said, "Harry! By the way, thanks for the help. Dropping that glass was a pretty dangerous thing to do."

Harry just smiled and walked out the door. Luke didn't have the heart to tell him it wasn't necessary; he'd had everything under control.

Luke had Gunther and Miguel come down and collect the saddletramps' horses, rigs, guns, and personal effects.

Luke didn't want to know what they found because he was now a US marshal just doing his job.

Early the next morning Marshal Simms rode into Taos. He had already been alerted to the excitement in town the day before and the way Luke had handled the situation. He headed straight for Luke's ranch. Luke saw him coming up the hill and had Star bring another cup of coffee and a plate of cinnamon biscuits out to the porch. Luke loved her cinnamon biscuits.

When Simms stepped down from his horse, he had that big smile on his face that Luke was getting used to. He took a deep breath and said there's nothing like comin' back home. Been thinkin' 'bout a cup of Miss Star's good coffee fer two days. Do I smell cinnamon buns?"

Luke handed him a cup, and they both sat down in a rocker and talked about the saddletramps and their demise. Marshal Simms told Luke that he had done a good job, just as he knew he would. An hour or so later Brady Simms headed back down the hill to check his telegrams and his office.

Later that morning Luke, Morning Star, Bear, Storm, and the big grey went for a ride up the mountain. They picked apples and gave the horses their fair share and let them graze on sweet grass as Luke and Star looked over the valley and their land. On the way back down the mountain, Luke said he was going into town to check in with Marshal Simms.

When he walked into the marshal's office he could see there was a problem.

"What's up?" Luke asked, and the marshal looked at him with dread in his eyes.

"I have a problem over Silver City way. Seems some bad guys are makin' the miners' lives miserable. Three have been killed and robbed, and several have been beat and robbed on the way to town with their ore."

Luke replied, "Ya know, I'm kinda tired of sittin' around this place. I wouldn't mind getting back on the trail again. Whatdaya say Star and me take a little ride over to Silver City and see what we can do to help?"

"Are you sure?" asked the marshal.

"You need some help, and I thought that's what ya made me a marshal for. Say the word and we'll be on our way."

"When can ya leave?" asked Brady.

"How 'bout first thing in the morning unless you need me to go sooner?" asked Luke.

Brady smiled.

"That would sure take a load off my mind."

The next morning about an hour before sunrise, the wagon and ox cart was provisioned up, and Luke and Morning Star headed the mules and wagons down the hill to the main trail with Storm and Bear following close behind and Star's big grey tied to the cart. They moved fast and steady, and by late afternoon they were within twenty miles of Santa Fe.

Luke loved being back on the trail and out of doors with his love and best friends and he was looking forward to the new adventure.

The End.

Follow new US Marshal Luke Kash, Morning Star, Bear, and Storm in the new Luke Kash Western, *Spirit and the Blood*, coming soon.